the REUNION

JOHN R. WILLIAMS

RY PUBLISHING

Xpress Yourself Publishing, LLC
P. O. Box 1615
Upper Marlboro, Maryland 20773

All Xpress Yourself Publishing titles are available at special quantity discounts for bulk purchases for sales, promotions, premiums, fund-raising, educational or institutional use by calling 301-390-3645.

ISBN-10: 0-9818094-4-8
ISBN-13: 978-0-9818094-4-1

Library of Congress Control Number: 2009921878

Printed in the United States of America

Cover Design and Interior Layout by The Writer's Assistant
www.thewritersassistant.com

Visit Xpress Yourself Publishing online:
www.XpressYourselfPublishing.org

the
REUNION

JOHN R. WILLIAMS

Chapter 1

"Sean, make love to me; right here and right now," she whispered to me, and then closed her eyes. I slowly undressed her, taking my time and enjoying what I felt and saw.

"Kiss me, Sean."

Obliging her request, I kissed her passionately, and her feet left the floor, her legs wrapped tightly around my waist. I carried her to the bed. Easing her legs from around my waist, my lover unbuttoned my shirt and unfastened my belt buckle, as I reached under her dress, and caressed her thighs, before removing the red thong she wore. Impatient and wanting to feel her, I gently grazed my thumb between her thick lips.

"*Oooh shit*, baby," she moaned. "That feels *so* damn good to me," my sweetheart moaned, sounding like a love angel.

I hummed in my low register and told her how much I cared about her, my fingers now gradually stroking the inside of her. With her head thrown back, and eyes closed, she slowly worked her hips on the girth of my fingers, simulating what she would do with my dick. We kissed aggressively. I felt my nature rise. I could no longer keep my beast caged. Juices moistened my member, as tiny droplets of pre-cum oozed from my erect dick. The front of my boxers absorbed every drop, but not for long. My vixen ripped off my shirt and buttons flew everywhere, exposing my chest. She rubbed her fingernails across my pectorals.

"Look at you, Sean! You look so good to me."

"Thank you, baby, but I am nothing compared to you."

We removed every article of each other's clothing until we stood naked, taking in one another's magnificence. We stood there for what seemed like hours admiring each other's intricacies. I loved her small waistline and the way her back arched when she poked her chest out and locked her knees. Her nipples were dark and full. My black skin blended perfectly against her cocoa skin. Everything about her body was placed perfectly, even the tiny dots that surrounded her areolas. She was my princess. Her strong jaw-line and full lips complemented her face. Every time she licked her lips, I grew in anticipation. She puckered them out as if she wanted to be fed. I kissed her again.

I loved the way her lips looked on her face, as if God took extra time and drew them on Himself. The cute little mole on the right side of her face made her seem even more seductive. I wanted to taste her, feel her, kiss her, hug her and please her until she could take no more. I would make love to her until night turned into day.

She looked at me like a vulture. I was her prey. She climbed off the bed and circled me as if I was her meal. I was both confident and terrified. Was I enough for her? Could I satisfy her? Would she enjoy it as much as I would?

Stopping behind me, she leaned in close and pressed her moist lips against my back, and then ran her tongue up and down my vertebrae. She was such a mosaic with her freakiness. Wrapping her hands around my penis, she stroked me down with the pre-cum. I reached for my condoms.

"You won't need those for a while, Sean. I want to taste you. Feed me."

I was so turned on; her teasing made me throb with antici-pation. Like a snake, she slithered down my body, opened her mouth and accepted me. Her warm mouth was welcoming. She teased the tip of my dick with her tongue. It felt so good. I spoke to her in an intoxicated language of adoration that was only un-derstandable to a sex-crazed lush.

"You look so beautiful to me, baby."

"Mmmmm…You *taste* so beautiful to me."

"How does it taste?"

"Your flavor is warm and smooth like hot chocolate."

I was completely smitten with her. She had me sprung. I was every bit of hers as she was mine. I gave her permission to do anything that she wanted to me. She force-fed herself.

The thousand thread count Egyptian cotton sheets felt nice. There was little friction. My dick was granite hard. She played tag with my tool and her tongue. She swallowed my magic stick with a senseless fervor that overtook her. Covering my dick with saliva, she slid my pole in and out of her mouth, as she hummed lullabies that made me so hot for her. She deep-throated me until my scrotum tapped against her chin. She was so into it.

I watched her as she pleasured me, satisfying me to the point of feverishness. She began to shiver; her body vibrated like a pager. My darling put together a half-broken sentence in the middle of servicing me.

"Ooh shit, Sean. I'm about to cum, baby. This dick tastes so good to me. I want to feel it deep inside of me now."

Her eyes closed, and she began quivering uncontrollably. She had an orgasm. Seeing her enjoy herself threw me into a fit. I wanted to pleasure her the same way she pleasured me. I concentrated hard on holding back my ejaculation, pulling my dick out of her mouth; I had to stop her. I felt all the precursors of an orgasm coming. My dick stiffened to diamond toughness, and I began to tremble inside.

I hoisted her over my shoulder and carried her over to the nearby chaise lounge. I plopped her down as if she was a bag of rice. I forced her legs open and buried my face into her delicate folds. My tongue flickered and jabbed at her clit, while her moans let me know that I had sent her into ecstasy. I licked every portion of her inside parts and sucked hard on her clit until she could no longer take it, sending her into another vicious orgasm. She was in a euphoric bliss. The look on her face said it all. She began squeezing her breasts and clinching onto the armrest. She held on for dear life as I placed both of her hands on my baldhead. I wanted her to force feed her pussy to me.

"Am I hitting your spot, baby?"

"Yes," she managed to get out through the deep pants.

"Does it feel good to you?"

"It feels like heaven, Sean."

"Feed me your pussy, baby. Make me swallow all of your juices. I want to taste your waterfalls when you cum. I want to taste every part of you."

She hollered at the top of her lungs. I watched her as her body convulsed.

"Oh God, I am cumming for you, baby. Ooh, ooh. Can you taste my love coming down for you? Can you taste my waters flowing into your mouth, Sean?"

"Yes, I can, baby."

I loved it. Her cum tasted like peaches. She had multiple orgasms from our sexy foreplay. She pushed my head from between her legs and slid her ass closer toward my pelvis. My dick was mere inches away from her opening. I grabbed a condom off the nightstand, tore open the wrapper and rolled it on with lightning speed. Lying in a submissive position, I leaned in close and whispered into her ear.

"Baby, I love you so much. I want to enjoy every moment of this."

"Me too, Sean, I want to feel you inside of my soul, baby. We owe this moment to ourselves."

I readjusted my body. She was spread-eagle, waiting for me. As I looked at her, I visualized my rod sliding in and out of her. My dick was just the right size for her juicy love spot. I knew I was thick enough to stretch her sugar walls and stroke against her G-spot.

I grabbed her plump bottom and filled her out with my dick, her breasts sitting up on her chest and swaying from side. I nibbled on her neck and kissed her gently. She spoke to me.

"I want you to make love to me first; then I want you to fuck me."

"I love you, baby."

"I love you too, Sean."

I motioned towards her. I jabbed the tip of my penis against her clit and searched for a warm, wet home. Jade begged me to insert, but I waited. I was still. I wanted her to want me as bad as I wanted her. I needed her to crave for me.

"Put it inside of me, baby; I need to feel you."

In one action and with no stillness, I fully inserted every bit of my tool inside inch by inch. She held on for dear life. I shook vehemently from her warmth. We both took deep breaths.

In unison, we uttered the same soulful sounds, only they were octaves apart. Moaning in G-sharp minor and trapped in circle of fifths, our bodies were in the same key signature. It felt so good; it felt so right. For the first five minutes, we made love, then as she instructed, we spent the rest of the time fucking. She encouraged me.

"Now I want you to fuck me, Sean. Fuck this pussy! Poke me with that fat dick."

"You better fuck me back, baby."

"Sean, I'm gonna put this pussy on you like you've never felt before."

I pinned her arms down flat against the soft sheets. Her back pressed hard against the bed. I forced myself deeper and deeper inside of her. She met my every move and pulled her legs even further apart. Soon her legs were completely behind her head. I had only seen moves like that in adult films. Her ass was propped up like candy on a shelf. Her pussy was for the taking. I had penetrated her so deeply; I could feel the labia of her vagina surrounding my balls. She covered my testicles with her sticky lotions. She loved it. We fucked for nearly thirty more minutes like two dogs in heat. She screamed and so did I. We were so into it. She yelled.

"Aaaaah! I'm about to cum!"

"Yes, baby, yes! Please, hold it right there. I'm gonna come, too."

I concentrated hard and stiffened my penis veins with every pump so that I could scathe her G-spot with every siphon. All of a sudden, she stopped breathing. Her skin was completely flush. It looked like she was suffocating, her nostrils flared as she tried to suck in air. From the way her face looked, she appeared to be having the orgasm of her life. She was in complete convulsion.

I left my rock hard penis deep inside of her folds while she quivered on my pole.

"I want you to cum for me now, Sean?"

"Yes."

My lover climbed on top of me. I placed a pillow behind my head. She bounced up and down on my magic stick. Like a jackhammer, she rose her ass up and then plopped it down repeatedly. Her titties jiggled from left to right as she rode my dick. Every time her ass plummeted down on me, I was closer and closer to climax. Her movements were sudden and forced. She had me in a daze. I took the nearby comforter and pulled it over my face to hide my screams. She had me hollering like a goblin on Halloween. I was ready to release. She must have known it too because she started talking dirty to me.

"Do I feel good to you?"

"Yes."

"Do you love this pussy, Sean?"

"I do."

I hadn't been through a sexual hurricane like that in years. I was about to explode. She hopped off me and removed my condom, then shoved my exploding dick down her throat. She tasted me and encouraged me to fill her mouth with my semen. She wanted my essence to paint her face. She assured me that no matter where I squirted, no matter where my fluids landed, she would use her tongue to catch my juices. I could no longer hold it in.

"Baby..."

"Are you cumming for me?"

I exploded! As I leaked, my lover took in my fluids. She caressed my shaft and massaging out every drop. I was in euphoria. All of my pain, frustration, anxiety, hurt, throbbing and aches were now gone. I had never felt as satisfied in all of my life. I was exhausted. The down comforter felt like a patch of clouds.

"Sean, I love you."

"I love you, too."

Chapter 2

Sean Jiles

A day in the life of Sean Jiles would be rather phenomenal if I could subtract one thing—my nagging ass girlfriend. I met Eva Sparks during my senior year at King College. Her name alone was what initially drew me to her. I had gotten used to seeing it posted on the Dean's List every semester. Our school's provost must have decided against being discreet. Lord knows he could have simply printed their names in the quarterly directory but no, he wanted banners. Every semester the stars of academia had their names etched onto placards in our school colors of purple and gold. On most days, I ignored them, but those tacky ass things were impossible to miss.

While in school, I worked as a librarian's assistant. The gig was simple, and although it did not pay much, I really enjoyed it. Creative in nature, I loved surrounding myself with literature, music, and art. No matter where I stood, the classics were always just a few steps away.

Aside from helping patrons, much of what I did at the library was file books. It was a mind-numbing task. Filing books took real fortitude, but I possessed that level of uncommon serenity. It was a thankless job but who cared? At least I had one.

9

I can remember the first time that I saw her. Lord knows that if it were not for those tacky ass banners in the library, I would have never made her acquaintance. Eva Sparks. Even her name sounded mystical at the time. She was a name on a banner, but she intrigued me nonetheless.

We met on a rainy Friday night. My merciless boss scheduled me for a twelve-hour shift the night before, and since I had the least amount of seniority, I had to work it. I wasn't pissed; I didn't have much of a life anyway. Seeing Eva that night was the highlight of my evening.

I have never been big on fashion. When I went to work, I typically wore the same basic outfit--a starched white shirt, loafers, and pair of pressed khaki's, but not on that night. Instead of my usual outfit, I grabbed the first clean thing I could find that was in my closet. It was my laundry day outfit. I looked like a misfit. My clothes were mismatched. I looked like a lumberjack, complete with a green and black checker-pattern flannel, a pair of stonewashed jeans, and some tan-colored work boots.

To make matters worse, I looked really grunge. My head wasn't shaved, and my face was covered with stubble. I was in fashion chaos. It was at that moment that she spoke to me.

"Excuse me, sir. Ooh, Jesus."

I covered my face from embarrassment. Eva looked like she was more humiliated than I was. Her face turned as red as a stop light.

"Ma'am, I'm sorry. How can I help you?"

I tried to regain my cool, but I was mortified. I was so self-conscious because of my clothes. If I could have done it all over again, I would have, but there was no "do-over" button.

Normally, I tend to think of myself as a somewhat charismatic. In fact, sometimes I am even borderline smooth. However, on that night, I was the biggest loser on the planet. Even with all those cool points I had picked up over the years by *keeping it real* and wearing fresh outfits, I still looked lame.

Despite it all, Eva took an immediate liking to me. We hit it off right away. She even said that I swept her off her feet. We necked in public, hugged in hallways, and hit the town together. In fact, we were so into one another that we just bypassed the whole getting to know each other part and made a beeline to becoming lovers. The first six months of our relationship were the wildest and most exciting times of my life, but Eva flipped a switch. She turned out to be the complete opposite of whom I thought she would be.

Our connection began to grow sour when we began dating exclusively. Although I cared for her, I started to see the signs that we would not make it in the early going. On the surface, we had a great thing happening. We were both college graduates; we earned decent money; the sex was awesome, and we looked good together. If people only knew about all of the arguments we had, they would flip.

Whenever we argued, it was always about the three M's: moving in, marriage, and money. Eva earned a six-figure income working at a firm in downtown Dallas. She was financially stable while I was anything but. At best, I earned just enough to get by. My money could not even meet hers halfway. My paychecks were pathetic, certainly not paychecks that commanded any respect.

Eva exploited that fact every chance she had. She routinely reminded me of exactly how much more money she took home than me. Even though we had more than enough money to support our expenses, we still argued about it. I was no fool. We might have been talking dollars and cents, but what we were really arguing about was control.

Within the first six months of us dating, she wanted to move in together. I was not ready for that. Things were moving way too fast, and I felt like we were plunging in headfirst. Moving in meant that we were in a full-fledged commitment! Eva brought the shit up every week, too. She was all for it. She said that sharing the same space would bring us closer, but I knew better. There was still so much that I wanted to know about her before I tackled that kind of obligation. We needed to give our relationship time to grow. Eva must have felt otherwise; she had no reservations. That behavior made me think she was hiding something.

To make matters worse, Eva was already hinting on marriage. She told me that she wanted to be Mrs. Jiles by the time she reached thirty. She said that she wanted a big wedding and an engagement ring big enough to make movie stars jealous. Lord knows I had tried to iron out my differences with her, but it had been to no avail. Just when I thought things could not get any more confusing, we complicated things by ignoring the issues at hand and had sex instead. We made up constantly. The sex was mind-blowing, but the cycle simply repeated itself.

I had only found solace through my writing. There was nothing better than sitting in front of a laptop and working on scripts. Although I worked as a bank teller during the day, my dream was to produce stage plays. Since I was a little boy, I had dreamt of becoming a playwright. I had been writing short stories since I was ten. As I matured, my work matured. I wrote for magazines. By age twenty-five, I was published, even though I set out only to test the waters. I wanted to see how people would respond to my work, but my writing took off! I built a suitable following on the underground circuit and in no time, my books gained attention. After eight weeks, my book made the local newspapers Top Ten List. After that, books started flying off the shelves. People from all over the country started buying copies.

I shopped some of my material to see if I could get a studio or production house to bite, but I had no such success. The studios were not as enthusiastic as I was about my work. No one wanted to hear about love and romance. They only wanted mystery, suspense or horror.

I researched government grant programs and any other way to get money to chase my dream. Within a year, I sent off more than three dozen proposals. I never thought anyone would respond, but I was wrong. Last month I received the Madison Grant. The Madison Grant was a $100,000 annual award created for the preservation of the arts. Each year, five candidates who demonstrated high levels of creativity received it. I will never forget how it felt when I opened that envelope and found a check that large. They even included an award letter printed on gold leaf paper and a large plaque to hang on the wall.

Out of all of the applicants, I was one of the five that won! I planned to use the prize money to produce my first stage play! I could fulfill my dream. If I were lucky, it would be a success and a major studio would pick it up as a feature film.

Eva did not know anything about the money; she never even knew I applied. I tried telling her once or twice but frankly, she just did not care. She wanted me to work a nine to five. Every week Eva found time to bitch at me about getting a *real* job. She said that I was foolish and that I needed to get my head out of the clouds. She said that being a writer and playwright was unrealistic and impractical, she even told me to my face once that I was living in a dream world. Eva had no idea that I was about to move on to bigger and better things.

Nobody thought we made a good couple. My mother said that we were like night and day. I first thought that she meant we looked cute standing next to one another, me with my chocolate skin and Eva with her frothy-crème colored complexion, but no. She meant that we were each other's perfect polar opposite emotionally. Physically speaking there was no denying that she was fine as hell, which was more than I could say for some of the previous women I had dated. Lord knows I was horrible at picking the ripest fruit on the vine.

When it came to the opposite sex, I was like many men. In the beginning, I was all about the physical. As long as she had a cute face, a nice ass, and could take care of my needs in the bedroom, I had no complaints. Following that model yielded poor results time after time. I ended up with some of the most homely females known to man. Nearly all of the women I dealt with were either unemployed or, as they would say, "finding themselves." Abstract statements like that did not sound half bad when I was in college, but once I graduated, I pressed the pause button on that bullshit and acted like a grown up. I found a job, moved into an apartment, and took a stab at life. Although I did not want marriage, I did want a good woman to join me in experiencing life

However, in my family, getting married was a big deal; it was like winning the lottery. Getting married was the final piece to the puzzle. All of the men in my family were blessed with queens, and every one of them actually found women that possessed *all* of the qualities they were looking for.

I made a list of those qualities, most men do. The obvious traits such as beauty, physique, intelligence, domestic skills and class can almost go without mentioning. However, truly great women have the little things—the details. They possess patience, kindness, and loyalty.

Unfortunately, Eva did not have those qualities. I have searched my soul and could only come up with one reason as to why I chose to stay with her; I settled.

There's no spectacular explanation, no extraordinary motive, and no philosophical reasoning. Quite simply, I settled. One should never settle when it comes to love. It drains love's essence from your heart and leaves the makeup of your soul thirsty. *So why haven't I left her?* Basically, I am afraid. I'm not afraid as in terrified; I'm afraid as in too scared to take a chance at love to leave. For the past couple of years I let logic and calculation supersede my gut instinct. The sexual quenching and safety net my relationship provided kept me from leaving. In addition, Eva can get crazy at times. If I left her, I don't know what she would do.

Our relationship was cynical at best. There was nothing special about it. What we had was basic, ordinary, and plain. Over the years, I became excessively content with standard. Conversely, if Eva summed up things from her perspective, she would say the exact opposite. Life for her was a peach. She had

15

a great career, a nice car, a designer shoe collection, and the man of her dreams. To me she never understood.

We had too many *nevers*. We never cooked together or painted a room. We never had a coffee shop that was *our* spot, or restaurant with waiters that knew us by name. We never hopped on planes headed somewhere exciting with nothing but an overnight bag and imagination to get us through. We never prepared Thanksgiving dinner together, lit a Christmas tree or watched the ball drop in Times Square on New Year's Eve. Whatever that *thing* was that made relationships successful was missing from ours. It's no wonder why I chose to write. I have *plenty* of drama to write about. I have argued so much with her that I'm at the point where I don't even care that I don't even care. I am sick of wasting breath on petty shit. There were better things in life to focus my energy on.

One time Eva and I watched a home makeover show on cable television about a couple that grew tired of their dining room décor, so they reached out to the producers of the *Fix it Fast* show. The producers selected the couple's letter and gave them a free home makeover. A professional designer came into their home, presented a design plan, and redecorated the entire room. The design really meshed well with the vision that the homeowners had for their space. It was a homerun.

When the show went off, Eva popped up, ran over to my computer, frantically grabbed a notepad then began making a list. She wrote dozens of words and phrases furiously on the paper.

"What are you doing, sweetie? I haven't seen you write that fast since we were in lecture hall at King."

"I am making a decorating list; all the experts say you must do that first before starting any kind of remodeling."

"Remodeling? Umm, babe, what do you mean by remodeling?"

"Sean, let's face it; your dining room screams bachelor pad. You need a makeover…bad! If I am inviting my parents over to *our* place, then I need it to look acceptable. This place needs an overhaul."

I was shocked at her blatant disregard. This was my apartment. I liked it the way it was. In addition, I recalled her using the word "our" and if memory served me correctly, my name was the only name on the lease. My place was not a dump; it was eclectic. I surrounded myself with everything that inspired me. I had all of my favorite books, photos, and artwork placed strategically throughout my sanctuary. I had my favorite musicians rotating in my CD player, and each piece of furniture was hand selected to fit my space. Eva wanted to violate and ruin it. I could not let that happen.

"Eva, *my* place is perfect the way it is."

"Says who?"

"Baby, you know I think you are a talented and creative individual."

"Uh huh…"

"You finished at the top of your class."

"Right, right."

"You even passed the bar exam on the first try. How many people can say they've done that?"

"Yeah, yeah, but what, Sean?"

"Baby, you are going too far. You are getting a little crazy. First, you watch a show, then the next thing I know, you want to experiment on my place. Come on now."

"Sean, you are so predictable! You *never* want to try anything new. It's always the same shit with you. I'm trying to make this place look like a grown up lives here. Come on, baby, look at this place. It looks like a heroine-addict lives here! You can't honestly say that you are proud to call this place home. If I were you, I would be embarrassed to bring company over to this place."

"Eva, for you to assume that I'm not happy living here shows me just how little you know about me. I can't believe that you found something to argue about *again*! If you want to redecorate something, why don't you start with your own place? Better yet, why don't you start with your attitude?"

"I don't have an attitude!"

"Yes you do, Eva. It seems like you try to control me every chance you get. Why can't you just be happy with me the way I am?"

"Sean, I wouldn't be happy with myself, if I were you! You have been out of college for more than five years. In that time, only one thing has changed about you..."

"What's that, Eva?"

"The color of your glasses!"

"Eva, you are a mess. What *else* have you noticed about me?"

"Sean, face it, nobody wants your material!"

"So you've finally said it!"

"Sean, you keep writing the *same* bullshit, in the *same* style, with the *same* theme. Your books haven't been selling and

18

publishers reject your manuscripts time after time. That should have been some kind of a sign to you."

"That's where you're wrong, Eva. All of my work *is* different! People *are* interested in what I have to say. My work impacts people."

"Whatever, you are living in a dreamland. Making the Top Ten List doesn't mean shit if you're not bringing home the bacon. Think about it. When was the last time you got a royalty check in the mail that was more than a few hundred dollars?"

"Eva wait--"

"No, Sean, you wait! You haven't been featured in any major magazines nor have you been invited to speak on any talk shows?"

"Go to hell, Eva! At least I'm doing something that makes me happy and not wasting my life away sitting in some stuffy ass firm."

"Do you want to know why I'm at the firm?"

"Please, do tell."

"Sean, *this* is why I work at a firm!"

Eva reached into her purse, grabbed a handful of cash, threw it in the air, and then hit the panic button on her Mercedes Benz key to sound the alarm.

"There's more to life than money."

"Like what?"

"Forget it."

"You are such a dumb ass! Why didn't you take that job in New York? You have more than enough experience. That job paid almost a hundred thousand dollars, but you turned it down."

"And?"

"I am afraid for us, Sean. I need some stability. A companion I can count on, not some dreamer that can't even step out on a limb to redecorate his place."

I was shocked. Eva had to have been harboring those feelings for a while. I guess she couldn't take it anymore, and neither could I.

"Eva, I think we need to take a break from one another for a while."

"What? Take a break? I am unclear. What do you mean by break, Sean?"

"Eva, we are not in the courtroom."

"Mutherfucka, please! You don't want to rock with me when it comes to legalities. I'll eat your ass alive. I will turn into Queen Bitch on you quicker than a New York minute."

"Eva, do you remember the first thing I said to you in the library the day we first met?" I relaxed myself and spoke in a calm, charismatic tone, hoping to lower Eva's guard.

"No, I do not!"

"I said that you were the most beautiful woman I had ever seen in my life. Do you remember that?"

"Yes, I do."

"Do you know what I said to *myself* during that same instant?"

"No, you asswipe, I'm not a mind reader. How in the hell would I know that, Sean?"

"I said that you would be perfect for me if you were as beautiful on the inside as you were on the outside."

"You really thought that to yourself, Sean?"

"Yes, I did."

The Reunion

Eva stood there with this dense look on her face, dim-witted by her own childishness. She cursed me, called me names, and insulted me. As much as I wanted to fire back, I didn't give her the satisfaction. I believed that men needed to practice restraint. Life has many potholes. Sometimes one has to smile about it. There was no sense in me being angry and resigning from love and compassion. I only spoke the truth to her. The truth cut far deeper than a creative insult based on a lie.

"Sean, you never told me that. I never knew you felt that deeply about me."

"Eva, until recently, there were several days where I was sure that you were the one, but now I think otherwise."

"You know how my temper gets."

"Eva, please don't go there with me. You've changed and so have I. As beautiful as you are on the outside, your attitude just doesn't match."

"Everybody gets angry sometimes, Sean."

"It seems like you are *always* angry, Eva."

"But--"

"Let me finish, Eva. I've come to realize that you're never going to be happy. You are always miserable, even when things are going great between us."

"Sean, relax; you're getting carried away. Couples argue all the time."

"No, Eva, *you* argue all the time and I can't take it anymore. There used to be a time when I would overlook your tantrums and mood swings, but not today."

Eva began to cry. She was no fool. She saw that I had reached a cavalier point. I finally had had enough. I was at my tipping point, and she deserved no more consideration.

She reached out to me then returned a statement.

"I'm so sorry, Sean. You're right; I am trippin'. Oyin really fucked me up for life. My therapist said that when I get like this, it's because of him. It has something to do with Oyin."

I hated hearing that name. She brought him up every time it looked like our relationship was going to end in a break-up. Eva knew the one topic that was a soft spot for me, domestic violence. Prior to us dating, Eva was involved in a committed relationship with Oyin. He was from South Africa, and he was a real asshole. He owned a few properties in South Dallas and was pretty well to do, so he walked around with an arrogant swagger that was detestable. Eva told me she was head over heels in love with him. She even said to me once that she thought they were going to get married until one day he flipped out.

Eva said that Oyin was insanely jealous, and that one day he proved it to her first hand. Eva exercised with her girlfriends on Thursday afternoons. She kept a strict pattern of routine. Oyin knew this and was a master eavesdropper. He read her e-mail, listened to her cell phone messages, and even followed her around campus. One day Oyin caught Eva and her friends checking out a hot personal trainer at the gym, and it must have ticked him off.

The glance was completely innocent, but from what Eva had told me, Oyin perceived the act as disrespectful. To him, what she did was unforgivable. The next day Oyin snuck into the women's locker room. He knew that Eva loved to relax in the steam room after a hard workout. Oyin was determined to teach the little bitch a lesson about disrespecting him.

Oyin ignored reason; he brought a pocketknife and a bottle of ammonia for his rampage. His eyes were crazed, and the only thing on his mind was punishing Eva.

Eva, completely unsuspecting, said that she walked into the locker room, undressed, and headed towards the steam room. She said that she didn't know Oyin was waiting for her in there. He hid in the corner with his weaponry. He turned the steam temperature up high so that mist would fill the room.

Eva entered the space clueless. She had no idea a villain lay there sequestered. Eva said she found her a spot, threw a towel over her face, and then leaned back onto the bench to relax. All of a sudden, Oyin popped up out of nowhere and grabbed Eva. Before she could scream, Oyin punched her in the mouth and knocked her half unconscious. He hit her so hard that two of her teeth fell out of her mouth and onto the floor.

"See, bitch, you never know where I'm gonna be! You think you can get away with fucking around behind my back? Huh, bitch? HUH!"

Eva pleaded with him as best she could, but her mouth was full of blood, so she could not manage any decipherable dialogue. The steam room fog acted as a velvet stage curtain for Oyin's sadistic performance. He was in frenzy! He slapped her, punched her, and held her down to the ground. Eva struggled but she was no match for him physically. Oyin forced open Eva's mouth with his free hand. Eva was fell unconscious. Oyin flung the towel that covered Eva to the other side of the room. He propped open her legs and violated her. He climaxed then reached into his back pocket and pulled out a small bottle of ammonia. He had purchased it on his way to the gym from a hardware store. Oyin's actions were premeditated. He poured the ammonia into her mouth and onto her vagina. Eva's insides burned. She felt like a sinner baking in hell. What did she do to deserve this? Eva said she mustered up a scream that was so loud that it bounced off the walls. She said that she thought that she would die that night.

If it had not been for a nosey custodian, she certainly would have. The janitor heard the screams and called the police. Within an hour, Oyin was in jail, and Eva was in the emergency room.

Every time I thought about what she went through, my heart dropped. The one man she loved nearly took her life. I hated to see her in pain. Therefore, instead of the fussing and fighting, bitching and cussing, I simply withdrew. In the interest of time and spared emotion, I let my anger recede. I took an "L" and let her win the argument. Relationships are so confusing. I wish I could go back in time to when things were much simpler.

Chapter 3
Eva Sparks

A day in the life of Eva Sparks would be phenomenal if I could fix one broken thing, my boyfriend. I met Sean at King College in my last semester. He worked in the campus library as an assistant. I had to rescue him from that shit! What kind of man chose to work in a library? I couldn't be seen with a man that worked in a library. Despite his job, he was sexy and incredibly interesting. I had to have him.

Meeting Sean was a fluke. The *only* reason I was in the library that day was to peek at the new Dean's List. Every semester I fucked my way onto it. Men are so stupid sometimes! They fall for a pair of nice titties, nice ass and inviting mouth every time. I have used their weaknesses to my advantage since I was a teenager. Why not? Since I was never really book smart, I had to make ends meet with street smarts and common sense. I became a prodigy. I did my research in the streets to gain an understanding of the world. I honed my craft, became a professional liar, and got everything I wanted from men. When other students were waking up early in a shitty dorm room, sharing, I took bubble baths in a luxury condominium on the edge of campus. While other students walked to class, I drove in my shiny new convertible.

All of my professors were male. They had to be in order for my deception to work. Once I got stuck with a female humanities professor. I dropped that proud-hearted bitch, and I dropped her class quicker than a New York minute. I've had professors give me debit cards and blank checks. I am not ashamed of what I do. I have never pussyfooted around the subject either. Quite simply, I exchanged sexual favors my professors for passing grades. I have passed every class with at least a B since I was a freshman. I never studied, wrote an essay, or took a single test. I sucked and fucked my way to the top and reaped the benefits of my hard work. It was an even trade; I got A's and B's, and they had the chance to fuck an exquisite piece of ass like mine.

You would never know it from my appearance, but I had it hard. I grew up in low-income housing on the bad side of town. All the food I ate was bought with food stamps or some kind of government aid. I never had much, barely a pot to piss in let alone clean drawers. I was an only child, so I was always alone. I learned at an early age that a woman had to use what she had to get what she needed. Where I'm from, moneymakers called all the shots. The dope boys and the women who ran at their sides were the people I looked up to.

Some nights, I would stay awake and sneak peeks out of my window at those urban knights. Instead of galloping into town on a white steed, they drop up in shiny old school Chevys. Those sexy brothers used to step out of their big body sedans wearing all the labels. They always had on nice jewelry and people respected them. Most of the respect originated from fear. Drug dealers were notoriously volatile when came to violence.

The dope boys treated their women like queens. They were the supermodels of the hood. All the girls wanted to be like them.

We wanted to wear what they wore, be spoiled as they were spoiled, and get fucked by real men. A dope man's girlfriend always had a seemingly never-ending wad of cash that her sugar daddy supplied to her almost daily. I wanted to be that girl.

Back to the banners, I remember how gaudy they were. Our school's Provost, one of my regular clients, decided against discreet placement. He hung them in the library's vestibule near the front entrance. Those tacky ass banners were completely unbecoming of an institution with the prestige of King, but the Provost ordered them anyway. He even ordered them in the school's colors of purple and gold. I only saw the banners once or twice a month, but Sean worked in the library and had the unfortunate chore of seeing them every day.

Oddly enough, if it were not for those banners, I would have never met Sean. We barely had anything in common. Sean was an artsy type. He always seemed to be on the cusp of finding himself. We spoke differently, dressed differently, and acted differently. We both had very different ideas about what it meant to be happy. He was a dreamer. A few times, I had to step in to talk a little sense into him so his head would stay out of the clouds.

Almost everything about him was ordinary, even his name. Sean was kind of name that could easily be forgotten. There was nothing special or catchy about it. I had to admit one thing though; there was something undeniable about him. He had a swagger. He was tall, dark, and handsome. His body was chiseled and strong. He had midnight black skin, and the strongest hands I had ever felt. Like me, he must have had it rough growing up. He had a great smile with pearly white teeth that seemed to sparkle every time he opened his mouth.

Sean had a mystical presence. His magnetic personality was electric. Everyone he met felt this uncommon smoothness about him. For me he was safe. I can remember wondering how good he would be in bed. I wondered what his dick looked like. I wanted to feel him deep inside of me. I wondered what he would taste like in my mouth. I had to have a conversation with him to see what he was all about, so I let him approach me.

There are two types of men: those that you fuck and those that you marry. Sean was both, so I investigated the possibility of us. I was ready to settle down anyway. It was time to give up the life. To me, any man can be groomed into the perfect companion. All they needed were the big three: some good dick, a great look, and ambition. I decided to seduce him. I went into the women's bathroom, put on some makeup, changed into my four-inch heels, took off my panties, and drew up my skirt to show off my legs. I knew that if I wanted to land Sean, it would take a different kind of approach.

Sean dresses well now, thanks to me. On that night, he looked thrown away. His outfit was totally out of place. He was dressed like a lumberjack. It looked as if he had spent the whole day chopping down trees. He had on a green and black checker-pattern flannel and work boots. I could see his package through his jeans. I began staring from afar. The bulge in his pants made me wet. He was hiding a boa in those jeans.

I liked Sean right away. He was not a pretty man, not by damn sight. He was sexy as hell! His haircut was low. It looked like new growth. I could tell that he probably wore a baldhead, which I absolutely love on a man. His face had a five o'clock shadow that complemented his strong jaw line. He had dimples and high cheekbones. Although he was dressed like shit, he looked good enough to eat.

I walked over to introduce myself and saw him fidgeting. He looked like he was a nervous wreck. Shit, if I saw me strolling over in my whore outfit looking good with my titties practically spilling out of my blouse, I would panic, too. He looked me square in the eye though. It took me aback. It seemed like he could see right through me. He had some amazing dark eyes that pierced my insides. I had to know his name, but as soon as I could fix my mouth to speak, he interrupted.

"Excuse me..."

He had covered his face, bashful-like.

He smiled and showed me a set of some of the whitest teeth I had ever seen. His smile and those juicy lips that covered them made me even wetter. I looked at him closer and examined his physique. He had broad shoulders and smelled like chocolate. His ebony skin looked deep-rooted and sweet. I wanted him. I knew I wanted to fuck him within the first sixty seconds of us exchanging hellos. I couldn't wait to feel his body pressed against mine.

"Hello...Sean. Isn't that what your nametag says?"

"Ugh," he responded, nervous as hell. "Yes, ma'am. It does."

"Stop calling me, ma' am. Call me Eva."

He swept me off my feet. His boyish charm and good looks drove me wild. He treated me like a queen. He was patient with me and he knew nothing about my double life.

Fast forward to today. Now I love him, almost more than I love myself. We have been dating for a little more than a year, and I think it's time to move to the next level. Neither of us is getting any younger. It's fate. We're both college graduates; we look great together; the sex is remarkable, and although Sean doesn't earn decent money, with enough nagging, hopefully I can talk him into getting a real job instead of doing that writing shit. On the surface, we have a great thing happening, but if people only knew about the arguments, yelling, and screaming, they would think otherwise.

The arguments started when Sean refused to let me move into his apartment with him. What kind of bullshit was that? What did he have to hide? I was going to find out. He seemed afraid to take it to the next level with me.

According to all the magazines, moving in together was the next logical step in the progression towards marriage. All of the experts say so. Hell, I even read in a magazine that *every* woman should live with her man for at least six months before tying the knot. In one way or another, I was going to get Sean to marry me, even if it took a little deceit.

Chapter 4
Reunion Announcement

I ripped open the certified letter in excitement with Eva standing at my side. The post address indicated that it was from the Kensor High Alumni Association. Eva leaned in closer and occupied my last bit of personal space. Her eyes zeroed in on my special message and for a brief moment, we both stood still. I read the letter silently as Eva interferingly read it aloud:

Dear Kensor Graduate,

It brings us great honor and joy to announce the official Kensor High School Reunion for the esteemed Class of 1997. This year's Reunion Committee has accomplished what initially seemed impossible. After six months of planning, we are finally complete.

Now it's time to party!

Enclosed in this package you will find a formal invitation to the official Kensor High School Class of 1997 Reunion Celebration. The Kensor alumni association has never conformed to customs and the ordinary. Instead of a single night of fun and festivity, we are hosting a diamond jubilee. Your three-day celebration is filled with events and experiences that you will remember forever!

We will commemorate our milestone in the place that started it all, none other than the beautiful, electrifying, and vibrant city of Chicago. As you open your invitation, let the excitement conquest your mind. This will be an event to remember.
Cordially,
Kensor High School
Class of 1997
Alumni Association

The letter shocked me. The invite could not have come at a better time. Eva's emotional coaster rides had me feeling as if I rode the tallest ride in an amusement park. I needed a break from her to catch my breath and refocus. I needed to go back to the basics, to a time and place that was calm and familiar to me. Our weekly disputes had me weary. I hated living a complicated life. I needed to revisit simplicity.

Had it really been ten years since I graduated high school? Over the years, like many graduates, I fell out of contact with my friends. Time and life helped grow us apart. Other than my best friend Josh, I only kept in touch with a handful of folks. For me, that was easy to do. I lived in another state. Even though Dallas was only a couple of hours by plane, once I started college at King, I never really came back home.

High school was the most meaningful period of my life. I remember being teary-eyed on graduation day. I made promises to keep in touch but like most, I didn't. The odds were against us on that promise. We knew that between going to college, finding jobs or life in general, we could never keep our pledge.

I missed my classmates; there were so many people and so many characters. I wasn't like most teens; I actually loved going to school. To me, there was no better place to be. I could learn, do sports, be creative, and see pretty girls. I could surround myself with substance instead of bullshit. I took advantage and embraced the chance to learn. Although it was not a requirement, I read a new book every week. I took extra classes afterschool and attended free lectures at community colleges across the city.

Staying busy was a good idea. I grew up poor and things were hard. We never had much. To make matters worse, I grew up in a single parent home. My father passed away when I needed him most, and my mother was a workaholic. She regularly pulled double shifts and extra hours doing home health care. I didn't grow up in a palatial estate with acres upon acres of land. We didn't have a trendy condo on Chicago's Gold Coast with world class shopping at our fingertips. We didn't have an oversized brick bungalow with spare bedrooms that company could use in case they ever wanted to sleep over. We had just enough to get by.

I was a hard head, too. While my mother worked, I ran the streets. They were never nice to me. I learned quickly to avoid them as much as I could. Every day was a different negative experience. Corner boys ran errands for the neighborhood drug lords. Street thugs were constantly being hauled off to the jail for committing petty crimes. Juvenile detention centers stayed full with criminals in training. I learned the do's and don'ts quick. In order to survive, I wised up and learned how to stay my ass in the house.

Coming from a broken home hardened me. I felt like I needed to escape. I felt like there was more in the world than crime and punishment. Before my father died, I promised him I would not end up a statistic. I made a vow to him, and to myself, to outlast the storm and do something positive with my life. I wasn't naïve. I knew doing right would be hard, but I had to try. I refused to give up and turn to foolishness for quick cash. I could not end up hustlin' drugs for petty cash.

In no way was it acceptable to sell drugs, but I understood why those young cornermen chose to do what they did it. How dare I judge? When your stomach is growling and there is nothing to eat, you get desperate. I knew how it felt to look in the refrigerator and see nothing but the white light bulb that illuminated the inside. I knew how it felt to look in the pantry and see nothing but some dry beans, a jar of peanut butter, and a bag of flour. Even as a grown man, I never forgot how that hunger felt.

The old folks on my block used to tease me and say I was the smartest dude on the block. I felt too smart to fail, and even if I wasn't given a fair chance, I felt obligated to make something of myself. I could not use my father's death as a crutch. Although I was dealt a bad hand, I couldn't let temptation catch up to me and snatch my ass.

Despite the dangers of the city, Chicago yielded some of the most renowned intellectuals, artists, athletes and musicians in history. Chicago had been home to scores of influential leaders and professionals. There were beautiful parts of the monster. Chicago has an eclectic mix of ever-changing physical and social climates that make people want to stay. The city has the power to transform. If given time, the city, like a butterfly, can cocoon and morph into a completely different place.

The Reunion

As I sat in my Dallas apartment, I wondered if Chicago had changed since the last time I visited her. I wondered if the skyscrapers still lit up the night like a million firecrackers ablaze. I wondered if the breeze off Lake Michigan still moistened the air so that it smelled sweet. I wondered if she still felt like home.

I looked at the letter again and searched for the event date; it was only two weeks away. There was so much to do. I had to get airline tickets, pack my luggage, and find a hotel. I walked past my floor mirror and looked at my reflection. Thank God, I'd been religious about hitting the gym over the years. I looked better now than I did back then. I put on about thirty pounds of muscle and grew into my slender frame. For many graduates, it was the opposite. Stress, work, and life whooped them and made them age much faster than they needed to. Instead of becoming grown and sexy, they put on weight, got bad skin, and looked a hot mess.

I was not that guy. Staying in shape was important to me. Somehow, I kept off the freshman fifteen, hit the gym, and by sophomore year, I was lean and built like a tank. I wore my hair bald even though I wasn't loosing any hair. All of the men's magazines said that women thought that bald men were sexy. I brushed three times a day to keep my teeth white. I had a great job; I was a college graduate, and I was about to live my dream.

I could do exactly what I promised myself I would do, produce my first stage play. My script was almost finished. I only needed to complete the ending. Things were going smoothly; then all of a sudden, I hit writer's block. Although the ending was crucial, I could not rush it. With books, movies, and plays, people remember three things: the characters, beginning, and the ending. I had a great beginning, but the ending was dry and boring. It did not pop. It would not succeed at resonating with the audience long after they had left the theatre.

With Eva breathing down my back, it was no wonder why I couldn't finish it properly. Instead of using my energy to focus on the play, I spent it fussing back and forth with Eva. I needed a break! It didn't take long for me to decide against taking Eva to Chicago with me. As much as I loved the thought of having a nice piece of arm candy with me, in no way was I ready to show her off and introduce her as the future Mrs. Jiles. The reunion couldn't have come at a better time.

Chapter 5
Eva's Opinion

Was Sean seriously considering that reunion bullshit? Was he really going to hop on a plane and fly back to Chicago? What was the big deal? I never understood why people felt the need to reconnect with people that they knew when they were practically kids. What made things worse was that he was considering going without me.

Sean was *my* man, and we were in a relationship. In my book, *every* decision has to be run by me first. In my world, the man has to gain approval from his woman. Hasn't he ever heard the old saying, if the woman ain't happy, then the whole house ain't happy? What was so bad about hanging out with me anyway? Most men would jump at the chance. My bank account is large; I am drop dead gorgeous; sex with me is incredible, and I dress nice. Most days are good days for me. The only time I get crazy is when I am on my period, but what woman doesn't?

Sean acts as if he never has any fun alone. Every Friday night I permit him to go out. Even if it is just to happy hour at the bar on the corner, at least he gets the chance to go. I let him watch one football game a week, undisturbed. I let him go to the gym as long as he agrees to take me with him. I have never had to exercise, so when I am there, I mostly keep my eye on him. Someone has to make sure he keeps his eyes on his treadmill and not on the female eye candy, which frequents the gym.

Why does he feel the need to go to that stupid reunion? All he ever talked about was high school. He used to tell me how popular he was and about all of the crazy shit he used to do. Even more reason for him to stay here. Jealous women simply love to rain on a bitch's parade. They see a girl out there doing well, and they try to ruin things. Misery loves company. Sean says that shit all the time. They can't go it alone, so they try to be miserable with someone else. To them, it's much more fun when they have people around them that are worse off. It makes them feel better. I should know; I have been that person before.

Sean meant too much to me. I could not let him go. He was my first. Not the first man that I had ever had sex with, that is laughable. He was the first person I ever made love to. He was the first man that drove me to an orgasm with words alone. His deep voice was so raspy and deep that whenever he whispered in my ear, I simply melted. Even without his velvety words, he was as smooth as silk. Without even trying, he oozed a scarce sexiness that attracted many to him. His swagger was simply contagious.

To top it all off, Sean was awesome in bed. He gave it to me *any* way I wanted it. I felt like his dick belonged to me. What girl would let a ten-inch long, cucumber-sized dick that tasted smooth and ran deep slip away? With other men, I had to pretend to get excited enough to cum. Either their dicks were too small, they weren't rough enough, or they came too quick to get me there. With Sean, it was different. He took his time with me and held me close. He made me feel like a princess. When I needed to feel special, he stroked me slowly and gently. When I wanted to feel like a bad girl, he pounded me doggy-style and talked to me like a whore. Sean fucked me seven ways from Sunday. If I wanted him to eat pussy, he ate it. If I wanted to taste him, his dick was always rock hard and waiting. His dick could get hard at the drop of a dime. I loved seeing the veins bulge out the shaft of his penis. I loved taking the head of his penis into my mouth. He fed me all the dick I could handle, and when he came, I slurped down his love liquid like syrup. His cum tasted so sweet.

Aside from the sex, I cared about Sean. We shared many firsts. He was the first man that ever bathed me in a tub or made me breakfast. He was the first man to endure my wrath even when I clearly behaved like a bitch. He was the only man that had my heart, and the only man I ever opened up to about my past. Sean accepted me for who I was despite all the shit, and people, I have done. Over the years, I have had dozens of boy toys, all shapes and sizes. I have had black men, white men, Asian men, Greek men, and even Spanish men. I've done three-ways, dabbled with girls, and have been a dominatrix. I have fucked more people than I can remember. I have lost count it's been so many. I have thrown away more condoms than I have pieces of paper and have left my scent in dozens more hotel and classrooms than Glade aerosol.

I hate to love, but I love to hate. Hate has fueled my decision-making for years. No wonder life seemed dry and breathless. Sometimes I feel like there is no hope, even though some say there's always hope. Nonetheless, how can I embrace hope when I can't even understand it? Optimism is as absent from my presence of mind as sunlight in the midnight firmament? I embrace darkness. It never made me afraid. It never felt wrong, and it never felt like sin until now. Sean was my savior. I needed his love to stop me from damaging unbroken things. I have never been naïve. For years I knew I had problems, but getting help was too embarrassing. With Sean at my side, I can change. He is the key to fixing me, not counseling. That's what bothers me so much. All this time Sean has been a good little boy. He has obeyed all of my rules. Yet with the reunion approaching, Sean may try to break them. I can't let that happen, not by damn sight!

Chapter 6
The Argument

"You can't go!" Eva shouted at the top of her lungs.

My Bluetooth nearly popped off my ear. Enough was enough. I could not believe that with one day left in Dallas, Eva wanted to argue instead of sending me off to Chicago properly. Most women understood that arguing is the last thing you want to do with a man that is about to leave town. Instead of giving me a little last minute affection, Eva chose to pick a fight. I was burning the midnight oil trying to get my writing done. I was on my second cup of coffee at the Neo-Soul Café near downtown Dallas.

I had a few more pages left to write in my manuscript when my cell phone started to ring repeatedly. Every five minutes Eva's ringtone irritated me. Instinctively, I avoided answering, but after the noise became a nuisance to the other Café patrons, I decided to take her call. I went into the men's restroom, locked the door, and got ready for battle. Eva was going to get a piece of my mind.

It was late, and I needed to get home and get some rest. My special weekend was hours away. Eva had become a controlling bitch. She used her mouth to nag at me more than she used it to give me head. In a very short time, she went from being the first person I wanted to see to the last person I wanted to speak to. Becoming a pain in my ass was her specialty.

"Hello!" I said in a fuming tone.

"Why haven't you answered your phone, Sean? Are you avoiding me?"

"No, Eva."

Eva's line of questioning infuriated me. She was not the boss of me. I began to wonder if her behavior was a glimpse of what was to come. Would our relationship be this way forever? Imagining myself at forty with a bad heart and high stress levels because of her made me angrier and angrier. I launched back at her.

"Eva, you are not my mother, and you are certainly not my wife! I'm getting sick and tired of your bullshit. It is always the same with you. Your insecurities and pettiness have reached all-time lows. I don't owe any explanations to you!"

"Sean, I know what you plan to do! You're probably out there buying some expensive outfit to show off to some bitch you dated in high-school. I just bet you are! You're probably planning a sexcapade in some cheap ass hotel. Sean, I swear, if you stick your dick in some bitch, we are through!"

"Eva, how dare you accuse me of cheating. Maybe I need to be worried about what *you're* doing. I have been at your side for too long to deserve this. I have seen your good days, and I have seen your bad ones too. I've seen your highs and lows. You should know by now that I would never do anything like that to you. The very fact that you're accusing me makes me wonder about what you do behind closed doors when I'm not around."

Eva interrupted me mid-sentence.

"Sean, you are such a fucking pushover. Can't you see that bitches are snakes? All they want is your money and that rock hard dick of yours."

"Eva you are talking crazy right about now."

There was no getting through to her.

"Sean, think about it. The last time I checked, you were a handsome man that wasn't on drugs, wasn't in jail, with a job. You don't have a bunch of kids running around, and you aren't gay. That's all a bitch wants nowadays."

"Is that all, Eva? You think that's all they want?"

Eva was burning a bridge. It was time to take a break from our relationship. Maybe I would even call it quits for good. She was in rare form. Amidst all the arguing back and forth, I completely forgot about the time. I needed to get back home and pack.

"Sean, you are not as smart as you think you are. You prance around your apartment with that beat up laptop typing up that bullshit. You think you have a gift, ha ha, how funny. Your projects will *never* get off the ground. You need me, Sean. You are nothing without me."

"Eva, you sound like a damn fool! I knew that you felt that way, but I never thought you would ever say it to me. I always knew you doubted me. Every time I had a stage play, you had something to do. Every time I asked you to read one of my manuscripts, you always found an excuse. You didn't even have the decency to show up to my book signing."

"Sean, whatever! It doesn't matter anyway. Bring your black ass back home. We have a lot of issues to discuss, things to sort out."

"Bring my ass home? Eva, where are you?"

"I am at your place...wait...*our* place." She hiccupped.

"You are at *my* place?"

"Eva, how did you get into my place?"

"With a spare key, fool."

"But I changed the locks last week."

"I know where your spare was."

"You know where I keep my spare key?"

"Boy, shut up. Of course, I know where you keep your spare key. It's under the flower pot nearest the left wall in the back hallway."

"Eva, *we are done!" Click!*

I hung the phone up, hopped into my car, and sped down the highway all the way to my building. I made it home in no time. I raced up the stairs and threw open my front door. I hoped Eva wasn't in a crazed tantrum. She sounded as drunk as a skunk on the phone. I walked through my foyer down the hallway and up to my bedroom. I could smell a poignant alcohol stench permeating the air. I looked forward and saw Eva standing there holding a whiskey bottle looking like a hot mess. Clothes hung off her body, one of her breasts hung freely outside her bra. Her pants were unbuttoned and her thong was wedged all the way to the higher crack of her ass.

She was intoxicated; alcohol was probably bubbling in her lower intestine. I stared closer at the bottle and saw that it was one of my finest bottles of liquor. .

"Why are you in my house?"

"I'm glad you called me today and showed me your true colors, Sean. I am so glad that we had this little conversation.

It's finally come out. You are *finally* telling me how you *really feel*."

She hiccupped.

"Listen, Eva, we're finished. We are done. I don't want you to call me; don't text me; don't send me e-mails. In fact, don't even speak to me when you see me in the streets. We are no longer a couple."

Eva's eyes began to tear up, and she spoke in choppy wording, but I didn't give a damn. In the past, her whine and whimper would have sidelined me with guilt. Within minutes, we'd be snuggled up in the sack about to go at it. Not today, Eva had pissed me off. The fact that she damned near broke into my place made it worse. She mustered up a statement.

"Sean, wait...wait...wait...hold on. Now let's not overreact. I've been drinking a little bit, and maybe I'm a little drunk..."

"Don't blame this on the alcohol."

Eva paused then laughed

"Okay, I am a *lot* drunk, and maybe I was a little out of hand for what I said. Think about it from my perspective. You are going off to another city. We haven't had sex in a while, and I just got my period. Perhaps I am just being a little bit emotional."

"What? Eva, you sound like a crazy person. Give me a fucking break. Don't try to use alcohol as an excuse. A drunkard bares the true intent of her soul. Keep on drinking so I can hear more about the *real* you."

"Fuck you, Sean. You ain't betta than nobody! Do you want to hear the *real* me? Here is some honesty for yo ass! You remember the stories about my ex?"

"How could I forget?"

"You remember what I told you he did to me that day at the gym?"

"Yeah, yeah, yeah."

I hoped to God that Eva wasn't trying to unleash her sob story again. I was in no mood to be sympathetic.

"What point are you trying to make, Eva?"

"It was all a lie. That story, the whole thing was a lie," she laughed hysterically.

"What?"

"I made it all up, you stupid mutherfucka. None of that shit ever happened. I never had a boyfriend named Oyin. They never found me in a steam room."

"*What?*"

I was speechless. It seemed like the walls were caving in.

"That's right, you piece of shit. It *never* happened!"

"I can't believe what you are saying to me, Eva. How could you lie to me like that?"

"Sean, you are as gullible as they come. You are so easy to fool. I'm no angel, baby. There's a lot of things that you don't know about me."

What else has she lied about in the past?

I was in holy terror, fearful of what other details about her life were fabricated.

"Sean, I hope it stings. How does it feel?"

All of a sudden, Eva hunched over towards me and started gagging. Her stomach made weird grumbling sounds. She dropped the bottle of whiskey on the floor. I stood frozen in place, not sure what was going on. I didn't know if I needed to call an ambulance or an exorcist. Vomit sprayed out of her mouth and onto everything in its path. It came out so violently that it covered nearly half of the bedroom floor with one spew. The vomit looked thin and scaly like wet serpent skin. Eva looked weak. She looked like she was about to collapse. I rushed over to catch her just before she fell to the floor.

"You think you are better than me because you get to chase your dreams while everyone else has to work. You think you are better than me because of those stupid ass books and plays?"

I cut Eva off in the middle of her rambled exchange and cut our lengthy conversation short.

"Eva, I'm happy. Even at your lowest point you continue to spew hatred at me. You need to be thankful that I don't hit women, because right about now, I would knock your ass out. Look at my floor!

Eva fell silent. I looked at her flailing body in my arms and watched her fall asleep. She looked like a small child. At last, there was no sound. Just like that, the beast was at rest. Eva was the fuck out.

Eva had my blood boiling. I wanted to toss her drunken ass over my balcony, but I decided against it. She told me a web of lies! How could Eva deceive me like that? To think that for all these years I walked on eggshells around Eva whenever the topic of domestic abuse or violence came up for discussion. I was extra gentle with her. I cradled her emotions and always applied an extra coating of care whenever I so much as came within reach of her. Now I felt like a dumb ass. The woman I devoted myself to deceived me. The whole experience amazed me.

Eva was covered in vomit, and despite the fact that I was angry, I knew I could not send her home. She was pissy drunk.

Even if she could wake up from her slumber and get into her car, she would probably kill herself.

Even though she didn't deserve any acts of kindness, Eva was still a human being. I picked her up and carried her to the bathroom. I sat her on my commode and ran a steamy hot bath. Eva looked like a wet noodle sitting there. She nearly fell off the toilet seat three times. While running her a bath, I had to use my weak hand to turn the tub knobs, and my strong hand to hold Eva in place.

She smelled awful. I removed all of her clothes and placed Eva's sleeping, nude body into the bubbly waters. I used vanilla body wash and Dead Sea salt to clean off the filth she was covered in. I piled up her soiled clothing on the floor. With innocence and care, I used a soapy rag to cleanse her every crevice. I removed the bath plug and turned the spout back on to get fresh rinse for her body. She was clean and vomit-free. I lifted her slippery body out of the water. Eva only weighed a hundred twenty pounds. I slung her over my shoulder like a bag of potatoes and carried her to my bedroom.

I walked her over to the closet. I found a cozy set of flannel pajamas and slipped the pajama trousers over her legs. I pulled the pants around Eva's thighs and over her bottom. Angry or not, I wasn't blind. Eva has always had a cute ass and a set of the most amazing breasts I'd ever seen. She looked like she could be a video vixen or in one of those porn flicks. I shook off the lust and tried to think pure thoughts. I had to remind myself that I wasn't trying to have sex with her. I was only trying to get her drunken ass dressed. Eva lived all the way across town. Since I refused to let her drive, she would have to spend the night at my place. Spending one last night at my place with her would not kill me. I leaned in close to put the pajama top onto Eva's chest. I slipped it around Eva's arms. I could smell the flavorful essences of vanilla and cinnamon from the bath I ran her on her neck. Her breasts pressed against my chest. They felt like throw pillows. I couldn't help reminiscing.

Eva had a full-size chest and the most beautifully constructed nipples I had ever seen. They were almost too large for her small frame. Although her skin was light and creamy, she had these dark brown areolas that always seemed to be hard. I used to suck the shit out of those nipples. I felt like I couldn't control myself. I felt like my tongue couldn't help but tasting those mammary glands. I used to spank those mounds with my hands and almost choke on them. I shook my head from side-to-side hoping to jar the thoughts from my memory. I had to realign, because I began to get a hard on. Then I thought about how childish she was just a few moments ago and magically, my boner went away. Suddenly, I softened. I took a deep breath of relief.

Men won't admit it, but we are suckers for a woman in distress. A helpless woman with a nice body can be dangerous. There is something gratifying about fixing a broken woman. It makes a man feel like he matters. For the same reason, distress, drama, and theatrics are what drive a man insane. Eva's drama and distress ruined our relationship. That evening I declared to myself that we were over

I lifted Eva one final time and carried her to my bedroom. I placed her body on top of my bed and slipped her small frame underneath the covers. I had a king-size bed with a double down comforter. I was certain that she would get a good night's rest.

I then repositioned the pillows so that they supported her head. Other than a few grunts and moans, Eva was completely silent. I reached across her face to the nightstand and powered on my Mp3 player. I set the dial to my favorite nighttime playlist. It had all of the greats on it: Luther, Sade, Al, Teddy, and even a little Marvin. I listened to it every night before I fell asleep.

Instead of sleeping in the same bed with her, I decided to go to the living room and lay it down on my sofa bed. That was a smart move, especially since Eva looked so sexy and seemed so infuriated before she passed out. Knowing her, she could wake up and go ballistic. I needed to be far enough away from her to hear her coming. By staying near the kitchen and sleeping on the sofa bed, I reduced my chances of being burned by hot grits. I was not up for any bullshit kicking off. My hearing was superb. I could hear a roach poot, if I concentrated hard enough. With the way the night ended, all I wanted was a little rest.

I took one last peek at Eva to make sure that she hadn't vomited again and that she was still asleep. She was. I stared up at the clock and saw that it read 3:00 a.m. It was way past my bedtime, so I took off my clothing then fell asleep on the couch in my T-shirt and boxers. What a night! I couldn't wait until tomorrow when I could hop on a plane and leave all of the bullshit behind me.

Chapter 7
Chicago Love

I woke up early the next morning, took a shower, and grabbed my luggage. I grabbed my duffel bag and stuffed it with copies of my novel and some promotional material then snuck out of the house before Eva noticed. That liquor really did her in. It was almost ten o'clock in the morning, and she was still fast asleep. I didn't want to run late, so I hopped into my sedan and hit the road for the airport. I made it to the airport in no time. I parked my car and hurried to my terminal to check in. I went through the security checkpoints and arrived to my gate almost forty minutes ahead of schedule.

"Southern Airlines paging passengers flying to Chicago; please report to gate A-8. We will begin boarding in forty-five minutes."

I grabbed my carry on and walked through the crowded airport terminal. I was a plane ride away from what could arguably be one of the most exhilarating weekends of my life. Most high schools celebrated their benchmark in their alma mater's gymnasium with cheesy decoration and music. Not Kensor Academy, we were different. In Chicago Kensor always set the bar when it came to dictating trends. Instead of following traditions, our reunion committee planned a three-day celebration that included bowling, a social mixer at the best bar in the city, a formal reception in upscale downtown, and a picnic with softball near the lakefront. Each event was designed with everyone in mind. No one could feel left out with such an itinerary.

I hadn't visited Chicago in more than eight years. After graduation, I headed south to the rejuvenated third coast, and attended college in Texas. The decision for me was an easy one. I wanted to do big things with my career and with my writing, so what better place to reach for my dreams than the Lone Star state. As the slogan says, "Everything is bigger in Texas." Women wear big hair; people drive big cars; families live in big homes, and hardworking people like me, chase big dreams.

Although it was early, I wanted a drink. I needed something to take off my edge. Nothing did the trick better than a few shots of good brown liquor. Too bad I didn't have time. On my way to my gate, I passed a bar that looked like they had top shelf. The bar was located catty-cornered from where I was to board my plane. I couldn't see inside of the bar perfectly, but I could see well enough to check out these two honeys sitting at the bar. Normally I was not a nosey man, but the two women commanded my attention. Although there were at least a dozen people that walked through my line of sight, I could see faint images of their physiques. Both women had long hair and were dressed in business attire. One woman had a light-skinned complexion like my ex, and the other woman had an ebony colored complexion that was as dark as wet plum skin.

They each had on oversized sunglasses that one would see on any Hollywood actress, and they both sat at the bar with drinks in front of them.

Both women looked good, but there was something special about the dark woman. The dark woman had a brilliance about her that seemed approachable. She was voluptuous with oversized legs, thick thighs, and luscious child bearing hips. The light-skinned woman looked angry and in disarray. During the few moments in which I stared, she never smiled. From the way she pointed her index finger and rolled her neck at the bar, I figured her to be an overworked, overstressed explosion that was ready to pop.

The chocolate colored woman was the exact opposite. She seemed to have an electric personality that commanded respect. I stared at her, mouth agape. While I could not make out all of her features, I did notice a deep dimple in her right cheek. How cute. I tried to focus in closer but was startled by the airport PA system.

"Southern Airlines paging all passengers headed to Chicago. Please proceed to Gate A-8 for boarding. We are now boarding at this time."

I searched for my boarding pass. I checked the inside of blazer pocket and found it. I took one last look at the black beauty and moved towards my gate, which was 3E. I looked forward to my flight. I always flew coach. Unlike my girlfriend who swears up and down that coach seating is for losers, I liked coach seating. All of the best conversations occurred in coach. On one occasion, a man headed to Vegas in search of his true love told me his story. He told me that he cashed in his 401k, sold his house, all in hopes of reconnecting with the love of his life. After twenty years, he still loved her just as deeply and unwavering as he did when they first met. After searching high and low for her, he finally found her. She worked on the wait staff at a restaurant in Caesar's Palace. They separated during a bad hurricane and for nearly twenty years, he thought that she was dead. He saw her in a photo in a gaming magazine and said that at that moment he knew exactly what he had to do.

I never heard stories like that riding first class. The first class stories were all the same. Either they talked about their summer homes in The Hamptons or stock tips. How boring! I walked into the narrow hallway leading to the plane. I located my seat, sat down, and secured my seat belt. After the flight crew completed their safety demonstration, we took to the air. I ordered a whiskey, snuggled into my seat and isolated myself. I trapped myself in thought, contemplation far from reality and passengers. I drank until my every breath smelled of fine alcohol.

The flight attendant offered me a pillow, and I accepted her gift. I located a tranquil place. The ground below became smaller and smaller as we ascended higher and higher. Soon my mind forgot all about Texas and focused on the Windy City. I asked for a notepad and pen. The steward was a doll. She brought me back my items along with another whiskey sour to help me relocate my buzz. I jotted down ideas, thoughts, and conclusions about my life, my manuscript, and my forthcoming play. I had lots of unfinished business in Chicago. In order to give oneself a chance at a positive future, one must first overcome a negative past. I needed to gain closure with people, situations, and instances from my past. I left so many doors open. They were like thorns in my side.

I whipped out my Mp3 player, which I kept filled with all the best songs. My songs were as varied, diverse, and as magical as my personality. Within seconds, I could escape to that perfect place. If I wanted jazz, I could hear Oscar Peterson and Miles Davis. If I wanted something thought provoking, I could listen to M'Shell Ndegeocello or some of my old Billie Holiday recordings. If I wanted to groove to hip-hop, Jigga or a little Mr. West never failed.

I needed something mellow for my flight. Nothing said grown and sexy like Maxwell, Kindred or Gaopele. I scrolled through my Mp3 and found the perfect play list; I titled the playlist *Emotions*. At thirty thousand feet, I sedated myself to the velvety sounds of Neo-Soul. They sung me lullabies and damned near sent me to dreamland. As the cloudy skies hypnotized me, I prepared myself for Chicago.

Chapter 8
On the Prowl

I made it to the airport a full hour before my flight's departure time. Before I left Sean's apartment, I hacked into his email and found his flight number, airline, and departure time. There was no doubt that Sean had me open. His patience, charm, and good dick captured my heart and held my attention. I talked shit to him, but I was no fool. He was the first man that I could actually see myself marrying. He could have anything he wanted from me; all he had to do was ask. I would be damned if he broke my heart by actin' the fool at the reunion. Folks tended to get crazy at class reunions. Booze and awkward moments make for lethal combinations. I couldn't let Sean give away my goodies!

I drove to the airport and parked my car in the remote parking area hidden from plain view. I could not chance running into Sean. That would foil my plan. If he saw me, he surely would go off the deep end. The way I figured, what he didn't know couldn't hurt him. For the sake of our relationship, I needed to save us and keep our shit in tact. He said that our relationship was over, but I refused to believe him. Sean wasn't thinking straight we he decreed it. He didn't mean it. All I had to do was show him how much he needed me, and he would take me back.

By sheer irony, my flight to Chicago departed exactly eighteen minutes after Sean's. I scrambled to the airport, hopped out of my car, and headed towards my terminal. I made sure I was careful, moving as steady as a watchmaker's hand. I did not want to be found out.

I forced myself to pack light; I only took a duffle bag. I filled it with panties, a few toiletries, and a couple of outfits. Everything else I would get from department stores. If I only took a few things, I could carry my bags on instead of checking them in at the counter.

I strolled across the polished flooring of the main terminal and looked for Sean's gate. While walking, I spotted a few taverns on my way. I made mental note of their locations so I could double back for some spirits. A budding alcoholic, I needed a stiff drink every few hours in order to keep my nerves calm.

My girlfriend told me I was insane. She said that going to Chicago was a bad idea, but who in the hell was she to offer me advice on keeping a man when she didn't even have one herself? That bitch couldn't get free drinks at a bar, let alone keep her coochie filled with good dick. She had *zero* to say in the matter. As far as I was concerned, going to Chicago wasn't a bad idea at all. In fact, it was a brilliant idea, especially on such short notice. Who else would keep Sean in line?

I finally made it to Sean's gate. I kept my distance but could still see him from where I stood. As passer-bys bumped my shoulders, I tried to stay hidden amidst the surroundings. I put on a pair of oversized shades to hide my face. I walked back to the bar I had seen before and was pleased that I was still in plain view of Sean. I couldn't risk him sighting me. I took a seat on the furthest stool from the back of the bar in attempt of secluding myself. I placed my purse and duffle bag on the stool next to me instead of on the floor. *Who cared if I took up a whole seat unnecessarily? Bitch, I'm me!* I snacked on beer nuts and corn chips to calm my nerves. Despite me having on shades, the bartender must have seen the underhandedness in my eyes.

"Good day, sweetheart. What can I get cha'?"

"Excuse me?" I said in a leave-me-the-hell-alone tone.

"What drink can I get you, as in what type of beverage?"

"Mango martini, extra dry please."

The bartender scurried behind the counter and made my drink. I saw him fumbling the half-empty bottles of vodka, damned near dropping each one as he went along. Eager patrons ordered their drinks. Judging from the oversized goblet filled with dollar bills, the bartender had been working hard. He brought my liquid courage back to me, and I sipped it slowly, almost as if I was trying to stop time with my good liquor.

Another woman, sitting a few stools away from me, ordered the same drink I did. It was rather odd; I thought I was the only woman on earth that loved mango martinis. They were fabulous. The drink was sweet enough to chase liquor but strong enough to give you a good buzz. Who was she to order my drink?

I wasn't attracted to women, but I could not help but notice this vixen's physique. She was built like a stallion. She had dark brown skin that was flawless. She didn't wear much make up, just enough to accentuate her best features. Although she was seated I could tell that she was rather tall for a woman, at least five-ten, maybe even six feet.

In between keeping my eyes on Sean, I glanced over at this mysterious woman repeatedly. I checked out her vibe. She had a lovely smile and sat upright with perfect posture. She sounded educated, looked smart, and was well-spoken. She had to be a professional. When she spoke to the bartender, she used medical terms like psychosis, malpractice, and deterrent. *Only doctors use words like that in regular conversation.*

This woman had a swagger about herself. She had soul. Tucked under her arm was the latest edition of *Ebony* and *Jet* magazines. She sipped her liquor slowly, and savored its taste fully. All the men in the bar drooled over her. She quickly became the object of affection for many of the half-sober men in the bar.

I wondered what her life was like. I wondered where she was from and where she was headed. I wanted to know what it was like to be her. I had always been jealous of women with darker skin. People say that men prefer light-skinned sisters, but in my experience, men always preferred the dark cherry. I heard a man once say that *nothing* was more stunning than an ebony-colored woman. He said that their dark skin spoke volumes. To him dark skin was sexy as hell and never out of style.

Even though my skin was as yellow as the sunshine, I knew I had it going on. Frankly, I was tired of that bitch hogging all of *my* attention. I had to regain some of my glam. I removed my overcoat and exposed my voluptuous breasts. Grant it, the woman at the bar had the legs and ass of a thoroughbred, but I had breasts that could stop a train. My breasts were the one advantage I had over her. My breasts were D-cups, nearly twice the size of hers. Any man who saw them stared at them like infants waiting on their next feeding. To get the attention I deserved, I had to use what I had to my advantage.

In my mind, I was the baddest bitch in the airport, and I would prove it. I took one last glance at Sean from afar then took a bathroom break. I had to readjust my outfit and show off enough cleavage to get my way. While in the restroom, I unbuttoned the first few buttons on my blouse. My breasts nearly spilled out of my shirt. I glanced at my reflection in the mirror; *damn I'm fine!*

My bladder was about to burst, so I went into a stall and took a quick piss to let the alcohol out of my system. I flushed the toilet, skipped washing my hands, and headed back out to the bar area to regain my title. On my way out of the bathroom, some loser whistled and winked his eye at me to let me know that I was the bomb and in top form.

I walked back to the bar and slurped down the rest of my drink then signaled the bartender for a refill. I checked for my dark-skinned competition, but she was gone. *Where did she go?* She was nowhere in sight. What a shame. I had suited up for battle, and she bounced. She must have smelled my excellence approaching and punked out. *Fuck her, more power to me!*

I sat back down in my chair and pushed my back out to accentuate my cleavage. I signaled to the bartender for a second drink. He brought me another glass of potion with the quickness. I could not help but notice how polite he was being to me now that my titties were hanging out. His attitude and demeanor was completely opposite now that my twins were exposed. He said "please" and "thank you." He even smiled at me once or twice. *Men are such pushovers for nice racks.* I looked down at my watch and then glanced over to the flight status screens across the hallway. Sean's flight was on time and would begin boarding soon. I reached down in my purse, pulled out my itinerary, and found that my own flight would be boarding soon as well. I had roughly a half hour to finish up.

The Reunion

I looked over to the gate and tried to see Sean amidst the crowd, but it was hard. There were so many people. Dozens stood there gathering their belongings in preparation for boarding. How could I spot Sean? I could not see him. I looked closer but still nothing.

I was going to keep my man! He could not stay mad at me even if he tried. Neither could I. I wondered if he knew he had that affect on me. I was crazy about him. Almost everything about him was something special. I was in love with him, and he was mine to have. No one else would steal my baby from me. I was going to make sure of it. I stared at him from my barstool and understood how love made people crazy. Shit, I had gone crazy. I was crazy about him and willing to do *anything* to keep him, *anything!*

I watched Sean board his plane from afar. A sigh of relief exhaled from my lungs. I finished a third drink and closed out my tab. I collected my things and headed out to my gate.

I stumbled over to my gate and waited for the boarding call. By this time, my titties were spilling out of my bra. I looked like a Vegas hooker. I fastened my blouse and sat down in the waiting area until the flight crew called for first class boarding. The martinis started catching up with me and drunkenness was gaining on my ass. I was ready for my departure.

"Southern Airlines will now begin boarding all first class passengers at this time. Please proceed to the boarding gate to be seated."

Just as quickly as I sat down, I unglued my ass from my seat and walked through the narrow corridor leading to the plane. The flight attendant showed me to my seat and offered me a pillow. I thankfully accepted. I sat down in my plush first class recliner and set my mind to dozing off. As I situated my body in the chair, I watched broke ass coach passengers pass me when they boarded. One by one, peon after peon, young and old, they walked through the narrow cabin and found their cheap seats. *Having money was the shit!* No way would I be caught dead flying coach.

My eyes hung low and sleepiness overcame my body. I repositioned myself and turned my head towards the cabin window. The outside world looked small. Once all of the passengers were aboard, the plane took off. The flight crew completed an emergency demonstration. As soon as we took off, I was halfway to dreamland.

I whipped out my powder press mirror and used it to remove my lipstick. I took one final look at myself before closing my compact. What I saw next in the mirror's reflection startled me. I looked closer and made sure my eyes were not deceiving me. Seated ten rows behind me, sitting in the coach section, primped up looking baby doll cute was the woman from the bar!

Chapter 9
Mile High Thoughts

My plane was finally about to land. I was so anxious. Due to delays, we had arrived thirty minutes later than we had planned. Normally I would have been pissed off, but not today. I had no worries. My slow jams helped me mellow out. I was no longer frantic like when I first received the invitation. Accompanying the invitation was a collection of photos. I could not believe someone dug up an old black and white photo of me in our school auditorium, with a script in hand, directing my first play.

I have always loved writing and directing. It freed me. I actually remember the first script I wrote. It was a project I called *Pensées Vertes*—French for Green Thought. The play focused heavily on relationships from a teenage point of view. I won an award from the school superintendent for the play, and it marked the beginning of something special for me.

The opening monologue read:

I allowed her to breathe into my lungs so I could taste her sweet intention. I kissed her with an unbridled passion that could not be left without. With sweet molasses flavored lips and pillow-soft skin, we were caught in a gradient of embrace.

I dreamt about her and the moments that we would capture and steal away from. Waiting, hoping, starving and all but denying the affect that she had on me. She was everything, unequivocally. Every piece of her was perfect to me. Every line, every shape, every part, every cell, every limb, and everything from the curve of her smile to the single dimple that rested on her left cheek was placed just right. That dimple, my Achilles heel, stared at me and rested on her face like a tiger cub in the warmth of her mother's buxom. She was ice cold, nothing short of an arctic wind during a midsummer night.

I loved her. She was what could have been but never happened. She was supple and yet yielding. Her kisses were strawberry slices on a hungry tongue; her sugary smell imprisoned me and stole away my nostrils in a rapture of seduction. I loved the way she made me feel. I felt alive in front of her. She made me feel. In every essence of the word, I felt her. She captured my attention, and in so many ways made time stand still. I could not understand how my lips were worthy enough to speak her name.

The main character in the play was a mirror image of who I was. Nothing special, he was just your average teen trying to deal with hormones. He was unique, because he had the ability to recognize and deal with grown up emotions even though he was young. His meager beginnings exposed him to a plethora of adult-sized problems, including drug addiction, broken homes, and a seemingly perpetual question of his faith. I splashed in a few crazy instances of common life, a little romance, coupled with the eventuality of an approaching adulthood, and had my play.

The Reunion

At first, I was afraid to expose my life to the public, but I gave up the shocking details of my life anyhow. I submerged myself into the waters of self-comprehension and allowed its magnificent cleansing affects to drown me. The play helped me to regain my focus. I soon found better ways to pass my time. In retrospect, the play all but saved my life.

When I wrote plays, I always created main characters that people could identify with. They were usually male. They were always funny, humble, and down to earth. By using those building blocks, my audiences never felt detached from the human aspects of the character. My scenes often depicted real life ordeals and occurrences from my real life.

Josh, a friend I met during my first year, always analyzed my work. Josh was an immense thinker, he scored a 2340 on his S.A.T exam, that was a near perfect score. Despite the aforementioned, sometimes he was just a downright silly ass dude. He always found ways to make me feel better about bad situations. He used his unique outlook on the world to help me see beauty in basic truths of life.

Those were the days. Although Josh went to college in Virginia, he and I remained friends. We kept in touch and spoke to each other a few times a week over the phone. We both went to college to chase our dreams. We were on a serious grind. As teens, we talked about making it big in the Arts. I focused on writing while Josh focused on music. After six years, Josh graduated with honors. Offers to perform on stage soon poured in. Josh had become the accomplished tenor he had always dreamt about. Now he performs in theatres all across the country.

I could not wait to land so I could catch up with him. Chicago would be the perfect getaway for my life. Between Eva bitching and writers block, my life had been tough. It could be worse. I needed some good R&R to avoid going crazy. While I sat there on the plane anxious and scatterbrained, I wondered what Eva was up to back home. I was so glad to get away from her. Christ knows she has been a handful. I am glad that I broke it off. No way in hell was I marrying her. She could be Lucifer's bride, not mine.

I was still a little nervous about her being in my apartment while I was away. I snuck out of my pad like a thief in the night with her hung over in PJ's. Did she trash my place? Was it on fire? *Who cared?* I wasn't going to waste my weekend concerning myself with Eva. Literally speaking, she was hundreds of miles away. All I cared about was having a good time at my reunion. Then the loud speaker sounded.

"Southern Airlines would like to thank you for flying the friendly skies with us. We will be landing in Chicago ahead of schedule. Once we land, the pilot will be taxiing for a few minutes then we will arrive to our gate."

Chapter 10
On the Chase

"Welcome to Chicago! The time is now 1:00 p.m. Passengers are now free to de-board the plane. Exiting passengers can find the baggage claim at gate B-18, again B-18. On behalf of my flight crew and co-pilot, Southern Airlines would like to thank you for choosing us for your flight needs. We understand that you have choices, and it means a lot to us that you chose Southern."

I looked down to my watch and as sure as a pig's ass is pink, my watch read 1:00 p.m. The early arrival gave me a thirty-minute jump on Sean. I could call that a miracle, but I didn't believe in that kind of shit.

Where I grew up there was no God. People were mugged, beat, and killed every day. I was a realist; I believed in the here and now. I didn't waste time believing in religion, but Sean did. So every time the topic of religious conviction came up, I played along. If Sean wanted to read the Bible, I sat there and painstakingly listened to each verse. Every Sunday Sean popped out of bed eager to go to church. I was the opposite. I wanted beauty rest. Each week I thought of a different excuse of why I couldn't go worship with him.

I would tell Sean all kinds of shit to get him off my back.

"I like my church home a little better, Sean. I want to support my pastor. Baby, go ahead without me; you don't need me with you to praise God."

My lies worked! Sean was a patient man, and I took advantage of him for it. He never argued, fussed, or got loud with me. He was super cool during conflict. I always felt safe. Sean had a way with words too. He used to say, "That's okay, baby. I'll go to church by myself and pray for the both of us."

I used to think that he was too good for me then I would take one look in the mirror, see my sexy body, and realize that was the furthest thing from the truth. In my book, we were a perfect match. Everything he didn't have, such as money, power, and respect, I had. Everything I needed, such as a good cook, chiseled body, and some good dick, he had. We were a perfect match.

Everything played out as I envisioned. Sean's reunion plans were about to get derailed in a major way. He would regret leaving me in Dallas for the rest of his life. Sean was going to stay at my side even if it took the life out of me. I wasn't afraid to get krunk in Chicago! Folks up North were not ready for Eva Sparks!

I dashed down to the rental car area, duffle bag in hand. When I got there, I was thankful that there was no line. I glanced at the selection and rented the cheapest piece of shit that was available. Normally I wouldn't be caught dead in a compact car, but I wanted to stay incognito. I rented a car that was the exact opposite of my style. Instead of getting a luxury coupe, I opted for the gas friendly hybrid.

I walked to the airport garage and found my rental. The clerk at the desk told me to go to the third floor and look for a red sign. I walked up the helix and searched for my car. While in passing, I saw the most beautiful black convertible I'd seen all year. It was a midnight colored two-seater convertible. From the hard lines and aggressive styling, I could tell the car was Italian. .The machine was flawless. I snuck a peek at the insides. On the interior there was matching black leather and wood grain. The car sat on custom black rims with low profile tires. I got hot just looking at it.

I continued to walk through the garage. I found my car parked around the corner from the convertible. I unlocked the doors and trunk of the tiny machine. I threw my duffel bag in the trunk and closed it shut. I opened the driver's side door and stuffed my body into the tiny vehicle. Once inside I studied Sean's itinerary. Based on the list, Sean had rented a car from Chicago Rentals. *Not if I can help it.* I knew what I had to do. I whipped out my cell phone, called Chicago Rentals hotline number, and got into character.

"Thank you for calling Chicago Rentals. This is Charlene. How can I help you?"

"Good afternoon, Charlene. I'm scheduled to fly into Chicago today for an event, but I've decided not to go. I won't need the rental this weekend."

"I'd be happy to help you. Do you have a reservation number?"

"Yes, ma'am."

I gave Charlene the reservation number. She placed me on hold. I waited. She returned to the phone.

"May I have your name, ma'am?"

"Yes...it is Sean...Sean Jiles."

"Umm, excuse me, your name is Sean, ma' am?"

"It certainly is!"

"Well, ma'am, we can definitely cancel the reservation for you. The odd thing is that my records show that just this morning you called in and confirmed the reservation. There are even extra notes in the record indicating how excited the caller was about the event."

The clerk was cunning! I had to act fast to prevent her from foiling my plan. I went into bitch mode.

"Excuse me! Who in the hell are you to ask me about my personal affair? That is none of your damn business!"

"Well, ma'am, there is no need to get loud. I apologize. I simply wanted to know if there was a specific reason why you needed to cancel at the last minute. Asking is part of the cancellation process."

"I don't appreciate you being so nosey. Just cancel the fucking reservation."

"Yes, ma'am, right away, ma'am."

"Thank you!"

"Okay, Mrs. Jiles...the reservation has been cancelled. Will there be anything else today?

"No!"

"Goodbye."

I hung the phone up. Mrs. Jiles, Hmmm... *I liked the sound of that*. There was a certain ring to it. I said what the woman said again a few times. Mrs. Jiles, Mrs. Jiles, Mrs. Jiles, I loved how the words sounded together as they rolled off my tongue.

How could Sean get around the city without a car? Chicago was a big city. There was no way he could cover ground on public transportation. Then I would show up out of nowhere in my rental, surprise him, and rescue my baby. He'd be so thrilled to see me that he would forget all about the reunion and our break up. Knowing Sean, he would probably grab me by the waist and rip my clothes off on sight! He would eat this cat and fuck the shit out of me right there on the spot. We would go back to his hotel room and get it on. I'd pull off his pants to find his rock hard dick staring at me dripping with pre-cum. I'd fall to my knees, pull my hair back, and take him into my mouth. I would suck his dick as if it belonged to me. I would let him explode in my mouth like a volcano, and then I would swallow down each drop like iced water on a hot summer day.

Then we would bathe together in an over-sized tub then fuck right there in the water. Sean would pick me up with those strong arms and fuck me against the wall and make me cum again and again. I would let him fuck me in the ass and fill me up with that hard dick. I would relax all of my muscles and play with my clit to make the penetration feel good to me. I would bounce my ass against his pelvis and take in every inch of him. He would say my name then I would make him cum deep inside of me. I would squeeze his balls and release all of that sweet nectar. Sean would be so in love with me. Then after he came, I would wipe him down with a warm rag and then stroke his dick until it was hard again. Once it was back at full attention, I would surround him with my warm vagina, and we would fall asleep within one another. We would be as close to each other as two people can ever be. We would enter dreamland riding on the orgasms of our lives.

I began to get wet just thinking about my daydream. I reached into my purse and pulled out the one copy of Sean's book that

I had. The interior pages had a photo section inside. There was photo of Sean that I loved. He looked sexy as hell in it. I haven't actually read any of the pages of the book, but I loved the pictures.

As I stared at the photo, the thought of Sean fucking me had consumed my imagination. I was ready to cum. I looked around the garage to see if anyone was around. No one was in sight. I hitched up my skirt, licked my fuck you finger, and inserted it inside of my pleasure spot. I imagined my finger was Sean's dick. I inserted a second finger, a third, and then finally a fourth. I almost had my entire hand in my pussy. My fingers felt meaty. Even though they were not the real thing, they would have to do. I thought about yesterday and how even when I was drunk and a total bitch, Sean cared for me. I even smacked him clear across his face, and he didn't lay a hand on me. Most men would have knocked the shit out of a bitch for touching them, but not Sean. He was my Prince Charming.

Sean scooped up my vomit and even thought enough of me to give me a bath, despite the fact that I was damn near unconscious. Even after breaking up with me, he made sure I fell asleep in a soft and safe place. I wanted his ass so bad last night! I would have let him do anything to me that he wanted.

I jabbed my insides fiercely for what seemed like hours. I stroked my clit repeatedly until I reached an orgasm. I shook mercilessly and came vicious like it was my first time. I took one last look at the photo and then regrouped. I had to snap out of my fantasy.

Chapter 11
Interstate Woes

"Welcome to Chicago Rentals. May I have your reservation number or your last name?"

I reached into my satchel, retrieved my car rental information printout, and gave it to the agent.

"Here it is, ma'am. Here's my reservation information."

"Thank you, sir. Based on the paperwork, we have you renting a basic sedan for two days then returning it on Sunday. Is that correct?"

"That's right."

The clerk looked puzzled as she typed keystrokes into her keyboard and stared at the computer. What was going on? The last thing I needed was to be without wheels on my big weekend.

"Is there a problem, ma'am?" I was beginning to get concerned.

"Umm, no, sir; it's just that...one moment, sir. I will need to speak with my manager about your reservation."

"The woman behind the counter went in the back office and remained there for what seemed like eons. I waited patiently but grew worried because of the delay. The people standing were impatient; they cut their eyes at me and called me names. The clerk came back to the front desk with the manager.

"Mr. Jiles?"

"Yes, ma'am."

"I'm the manager."

"It's nice to meet you."

"Mr. Jiles, unfortunately we seem to have a little bit of a problem."

"What kind of a problem?"

"Please call me Charlene."

"Okay, what kind of a problem do we have, Charlene?"

Although stressed, I still spoke to her politely as if I had home training. I made eye contact with the woman and continued our conversation.

"Well, sir, despite the fact that you had a reservation, somehow the reservation was cancelled."

"It was cancelled? I made the reservation myself over two weeks ago, and I even called in this morning to confirm it. The customer service agent assured me that everything was good to go. How could this be?"

"Well, sir, we are a little confused about the situation ourselves. Based on our records, I show that your reservation was actually cancelled."

"Cancelled? When was it cancelled? There must be a mistake in your system somewhere. Please help me understand."

I grew impatient. If I didn't cancel the reservation, who did? Who could have? There had to some kind of mix up or something.

"Well, Mr. Jiles--"

"Please call me Sean," I interrupted.

"Our records show that the existing reservation was cancelled because you were no longer attending the event. To make matters worse, we're totally booked. We are completely out of cars."

"Oh my God, this is not happening. I made a special trip here for this event.

"What event is that, sir?"

"Again, call me Sean."

"I am sorry, Sean. I was just being polite."

"Charlene, this weekend I celebrate my ten year high school class reunion. I wouldn't have missed it for the world."

"Really? From the look on your face, I can see how important it is to you. The only problem is that we are booked solid, and we don't have any more vehicles to rent out. I am so sorry."

"Charlene--"

"Mr. Jiles, I am sorry but--"

"Please, Charlene, just let me explain."

Charlene reluctantly agreed to hear me out even though there was a line of angry patrons behind me.

"You see, Charlene, I have been working fifty hour work weeks nonstop for about six months. I have been losing sleep trying to get my manuscript done. In a few months, I have to complete my first stage play, and I just broke up with an insane girlfriend who's probably trashing my place as we speak! In fact, she might have even been the one who cancelled the reservation. She has been trying to sabotage my trip since day one. I am begging you. All I want to do is get a car, go to my hotel, get some rest, see my mama, and go to Kensor's High School Class Reunion."

"You went to Kensor?"

"Yes, I did, Charlene."

"I knew you looked familiar! Oh my God! I don't believe it!"

"What do you mean? I don't understand."

The clerk left the front counter with her hands covering her mouth. She came back in seconds holding a copy of my first novel, *The Day My Life Was No More*. It was a first edition version.

"Sean! I went to Kensor too!"

"Really?"

I looked the young lady in the eyes, stared at her nametag, and tried to match the name with her face, but I couldn't."

"Sean, I went to Kensor. I graduated a few years after you graduated. I was a freshman when you were a junior."

"No way, I don't believe it!"

"Yup, my homeroom class was right next to yours. Oh my, you look exactly the same. You don't look different at all! Well, maybe a little, but in a good way."

"Thank you very much for the compliment."

"I used to have the biggest crush on you. My girlfriends and I used to go to your plays. Did you know that they still put your play on each fall?"

"No, I did not."

I was stunned; sometimes the world seemed so small.

"Sean, I'm sorry for the third degree. It's just that a little earlier I got a call from this rude woman and…never mind. I am so sorry, Sean. It's so good seeing you again."

The clerk and her co-workers were all huddled around staring at me with goo-goo eyes. They all looked like they wanted to jump my bones. I was beginning to get embarrassed from all the attention.

"Charlene, I hate to break up the trip down memory lane but..."

"I got you, I got you. Let me see here. If I just rearrange that, then move this customer, then type in the special code. Tadaaa!"

"Tadaaa? I hope that word means good news for me."

"It sure does. Here's what I have done for you, Mr. Jiles."

"I thought I told you to call me Sean."

"Well, like Janet says, it's Sean, but Mr. Jiles if you're nasty."

Charlene winked her eye at me as if we were in the bedroom and she was about to put it on me. I smiled but was still embarrassed from the previous exchange of words.

"Sean, I have re-confirmed the reservation for you."

"Really! You are a lifesaver! Thank you so much."

"No problem. It was my pleasure."

Charlene continued to flirt with me, but I ignored her attempts at flattery and refocused my energy toward getting the rental keys out of her hands and into mine. I didn't want to be mean. Charlene was not my speed; I was not attracted to her in that way.

"Sean, let me tell you this. We don't have any more sedans on the lot at this time, but we do have one car left.

"I'd take anything right about now. What do you have left?"

"It's a surprise. The car I reserved for you is a perfect complement to who you are. You are going to look great going to the reunion in it."

"Well, Charlene, let me say this; you truly have made my day, and I cannot thank you enough for all the help you have given me."

"No problem. Like I said before, it's my pleasure. Take these keys, go to the second floor garage, and you'll see it parked right out front. The car is jet black and brand spankin' new! Enjoy your time in Chicago, Sean! Bye."

The people in line grunted and watched me walk away a confident man. I grabbed my luggage and walked to the second floor garage as instructed. I searched for a jet-black car but could not see any in sight. I used the keyless entry system to sound the car's panic alarm. I heard the sirens noise. I walked around the corner and stopped cold in my tracks. Waiting for me in the garage was the most beautiful car I had ever seen. A jet-black convertible two-seater that looked like it belonged on a showroom floor. The care was perfect! It had a blacked out effect, complete with black paint, black leather interior, mahogany black wood grain, a black top, and black rims. I walked toward the car and my heart raced. I could not believe the car was mine for the weekend. I felt like doing back flips.

I unlocked the doors and popped the trunk to stow away my luggage. I threw my bags in the back, closed the trunk, and unlocked the car doors. Instead of the doors opening normally, they opened butterfly style. The car was certainly a rare exotic. I started cheesing like a kid in a candy store. I hopped into the driver's seat and placed my hands on the wheel. The crafted wood grain felt amazing.

I started the engine and listened to it purr. I turned on the radio and then reached into my jacket pocket to remove the special CD

I made for this occasion. The disc had twenty-five of the coolest songs ever recorded. I was ready to hit the town. I quickly put the car in drive and zoomed out of the garage.

I headed north towards the expressway. Interstate-94 was the perfect highway to experience Chicago. It led right into downtown. I cruised and saw sights I remembered from my past. Every time I stopped at a red light, people stared. It was all because of the car. Back in Dallas, I never got looks like that. I owned a basic late model sedan that looked like a family car. It had child safety locks, an ugly interior, and a dull grey paint job that did it no justice. Aside from a new radio, the car didn't have any cool points.

I pulled onto the on-ramp of the expressway, and no sooner than moments after I accelerated, I saw red and blue flashing lights twinkling behind me from my rearview mirror. At first I thought the lights belonged to an ambulance, but when I didn't hear sirens, I knew right away who it was; the cops. Police officers in the city were notorious for racial profiling. Back in the nineties, racial profiling was a huge issue, and it got even worse when the new millennium hit. Profiling was a reality.

The driver in the unmarked car began to signal to me from behind with his hands. He pointed towards the right shoulder of the road, almost as if his aim was to direct me out of traffic. I pulled over right away, because I didn't want any trouble. I was as clean as a whistle. I had no felonies, no convictions, or criminal background. I figured I would be fine. After all, I wasn't speeding; I didn't run any red lights, and the car was completely legitimate. I had insurance on it and everything.

I pulled onto the shoulder of the highway, rolled down my window, and looked for the officer. I put the car in park and reached into my wallet to retrieve my driver's license and insurance. Then a husky voice interrupted.

"Freeze!" the officer yelled. "Stop right there! Don't make another move."

What in the hell was going on?

"Yessir officer; what is the problem?"

"Step out of the car right now, sir!"

"Officer, no problem; I will step out of the car, but please tell me why you pulled me over. I didn't do anything wrong."

"We'll be the judge of that, mister. I don't want to have to repeat myself. Please step out of the damn car."

The officer drew his sidearm and pointed it at my face. I began to shit bricks. I began to question whether the man was actually a police officer. He was dressed in plain clothes and was not wearing a badge.

"Excuse me, officer, may I please see your badge? I just want to make sure you are truly a cop. I need to be certain that you work for the city."

The cop reached down into his rock n' roll T-shirt and withdrew his badge; it looked valid. I started memorizing the badge numbers and his name, in case I needed to report his ass later. The officer spoke to me while his partner poked around in my rental.

"Sir, do you know why I stopped you?"

"No, sir, I do not. Please enlighten me."

I stood there pissed. The overweight officer tilted his hunter's shades and holstered his pistol.

"So you really don't know why we pulled you over, funny man?"

"No, sir, I do not. Please tell me why you pulled me over."

"Well, sir, about fifteen minutes ago we received a call from a very hysterical vehicle owner. They said that someone stole their car. You wouldn't know anything about that now, would ya?"

"No, sir!"

"Where'd you get this fancy car then?"

"It is a rental."

Both officers burst out in laughter as if what I said to them was a comedy routine.

"What's so funny, officers?"

"So this car is *your* car?"

"Yes it is!"

The officers figured that there was no way that a black man could actually afford such a nice vehicle. Let them tell it, I was a drug dealer, a pro athlete, or a lottery winner. The two officers chuckled like overfed pigs then asked me for my license and registration. I removed my license from my wallet and told the officer that the registration information was in the glove compartment.

"Hand it here," demanded the bigoted officer. "Sir, we need to call this information in to check it out with home base. In the meanwhile, we will handcuff you and put you into a squad car until we can verify your identity.

"You are going to handcuff me? What? I am not going to sit in the backseat of a squad car!"

I was furious. The two officers seemed dirty beat cops looking for a score. Crooked cops planted drugs on suspects all the time. Who knew how many poor bastards were out there serving time when they didn't need to be?

The officer cuffed me and put me into the back of the squad car. I felt humiliated. I watched helplessly from the back seat as the two overweight men ransacked my shit. They marveled over the convertible and even sat in the driver's seat. They took turns placing their hands on the steering wheel.

One of the officers received a call from dispatch on their radio. I could faintly hear the conversation from inside of the squad car.

"Eight thousand fourteen to Officer Rogers, again 8014 to Officer Rogers, come in."

"This is Rogers."

"The license number came back clean on your perp. Mr. Jiles has no priors, no outstanding warrants, and no criminal record."

"Ten-four, and thank you."

The officer quickly hopped out of my rental car. He straightened everything he displaced. The officers walked towards me in disgrace, mortified from what they heard on the radio. The officer opened the squad car door for me and then spoke to me in a woebegone tone.

"Uh, Mr. Jiles...Sir...Let me get you out of those cuffs. Apparently, base made a mistake when they sent us after you. They ran your license and it came back clean. You are free to go."

"What? So let me get this straight...*base* made the mistake. You guys are full of it. Gimme back my damn license so I can get outta here. You know the *real* reason you stopped me. It's not because of the car, it's because I'm black!"

The officer gave me back my credentials. I hopped back into the vehicle and sped off. I took out my cell phone and called Josh. I *had* to tell him the bullshit I had just experienced

"Hello."

"What's up?"

"What's up, Sean?"

"I just touched down."

"Cool beans. I hope you brought some copies of your book and the manuscript. Folks are lined up for copies."

"Josh, hold up, man; hold up. You'll never believe what just happened to me."

"What happened? Did some terrorist shit go down at the airport?"

"Nah, man, my flight was okay. The whole airport experience was kosher; no issues there."

"That's good to hear. So what's up then? You sound madder than a mutha!"

"I just got pulled over by the po-po?"

"What? Why'd they stop you? Were you ridin' dirty or something?"

"Nah, man, come on now. You know me better than that. My license was legit."

"Well, if you weren't ridin' drunk or smokin' weed, then why'd they stop you?"

"For the life of me I don't know. The cop made up a bogus story about a stolen car."

"Stolen car?"

"Yup, they said that the car I was in fit the description."

"Are you serious?"

"Yeah, man. Those punk ass pigs pissed me off big time."

"Relax, man. Where are you now? Did you get arrested? Let me know if you need m to come bail you out."

"Josh, you're a fool, man. Nah, I'm good. I'm driving to the hotel now. I am about ten minutes away. I'm gonna stop at the hotel, grab a shower, then head to the picnic."

"Good, man. I will save a few beers for you then. It sounds like you need them more than I do. You gotta get down here to the park, man! Shit is off tha hook, playa! Man, everybody's here, and they are all asking for you too! Even you know who." He laughed.

"Man, cut that out. Is Jade there for real?"

"Yeah."

"Jade Brown?"

"Yeah, man, she is here and looks amazing! You had better get down here, man, before I snatch her up!"

"I'm gonna tell your wife."

"I ain't married yet, homeboy!"

"Well, you're about to be. Isn't your wedding in like a week or something?"

"Yeah, the wedding is next Saturday, but the bachelor party is tonight!"

"Yeah, buddy!"

Josh started laughing and kee-kee'ing on the phone playfully. He sounded like he did when we were back in high school. I could tell he was excited.

"All right then, man, I gotta go. I will tell you more about the police incident later. Instead of stopping at the hotel, I'm gonna run by Hyde Park Beer and Spirits to get the drinks."

"Cool, man. Sean, you always come through for me, man."

"Man, stop all of that. You know you're my boy!"

"All right then, I'll get at cha later then."

"Cool, I'm gonna grab me a bite to eat; I'm starving! My stomach is about to start eating away at its lining, if I don't grab me some eats. I will swing back to the hotel after that and just check in late. See you soon."

I couldn't believe Josh was tying the knot. He and his future wife dated back in high school. The same annoying, smart-alecky, red-boned, freckle faced beauty from back in the day had matured into an educated, take-no-shit talent manager for supermodels. She could have easily been one herself but preferred the business side much more. Literally, she managed four out of the ten African American models that were on the runways in the Midwest. Josh's girl had a hand in every fashion show held between Chicago and Atlanta.

She pioneered her signature bitchy attitude into a flawless negotiating machine. In less than three years, she became one of the most well-known and respected names in the fashion industry. She was a household name all over Chicago's fashion elite. They were perfect complements to one another. As busy as they both were, it was a wonder that they ever got their wedding plans done. Both of them paid heavy attention to detail, so they always disagreed about the small things. Since both of them were successful in their careers, they could afford the lavish specifics like a top shelf open bar, a two thousand dollar wedding cake, and a string quartet to play the wedding march.

Who would have thought that the same two arguing high school sweethearts would end up madly in love? If you counted the time they spent together at Kensor, they have been a couple for more than twelve years. She was the only thing that he knew.

Things are always so exciting when folks are young and in love; the romance is fast and free. Even with the occasional argument, there is no end to the ecstasy. There is no end to the passion. Then after a few years, that passion fades, lovers forget to appreciate one another. Josh and his future bride found the keys to love early. They were honest with one another. They supported one another, and they kept that fire lit. To this day, I feel like they were made for one another. I am sure their wedding will be a splendid display of their love, not to mention off tha damn chain!

Josh told me that he and his fiancée decided to do a destination wedding in the city that never sleeps. New York City would host the couple's extravaganza. As the best man, I couldn't let my buddy down. I pulled some strings, called in favors, and connected Josh and his fiancée with several of my Manhattan contacts to help him get good deals on the best space, catering, and entertainment that the Big Apple had to offer.

By sheer chance, Josh's wedding just happened to fall one calendar week from my arrival date and the class reunion festivities. More importantly, Josh's bachelor party was in eight hours. The bride and groom decided to have their soirees a week early so that they could get all the lusting for other folks out of their systems. They would have their last night of fun, wrap things up in Chicago, and fly out to New York early so that they could get things in order for their special day.

The Reunion

I took the nearest exit and hit up the first liquor store I could find. I went in and bought four bottles of the best alcohol they offered. I went back to the car, tucked the spirits away in the trunk then took the service road all the way to the hotel. I was already three steps into my reunion journey.

Chapter 12
Eva's Anger

I started up my car and headed out of the parking garage. Jerkin' off in the car delayed my plans. It was well into the two o'clock hour. I hit the road and took the nearest expressway to downtown Chicago. Sean's hotel was on the Gold Coast. I had never visited Chicago, so I had no idea how beautiful it was. Being in the city where my baby grew up was surreal. Thank goodness I opted for the GPS navigation system; it was a lifesaver. Sean told me that the highways in Chicago could get confusing for visitors. I sped down the expressway cramped up in my tiny box. I did sixty miles an hour, but it felt like forty.

All of a sudden, a car zoomed past mine. It looked like the vehicle I saw at the airport garage. The man in the car had to be doing eighty miles an hour. I recognized the shiny black exotic right away. Sitting in the driver's seat was a bald-headed man with chocolate colored skin and aviator shades on. He raced past me as if he was in the Indianapolis 500 I pressed on the accelerator and floored it. My wimpy motor was no match for his. I went as fast as I could go in my compact and pulled alongside of him. I was finally close enough to see the man in the car. It was Sean!

How could this be when I cancelled his reservation? Somehow, he was still able to get a vehicle. To make matters worse, he rented the best-looking car in the garage. Damn! I sped up and bolted into the lane next to his. I sat in my car puzzled. I could not put all of the pieces together. I wondered if he saw me. How could he when he didn't even know I was in town? I had to think fast. I whipped out my phone again and dialed 9-1-1. The operator answered.

"911 emergency; how can I help you?"

"Hello, oh my, God!"

"Hello, ma'am?"

"Oh God no!"

"Ma'am, please calm down."

"My car was just stolen. I was just at the airport waiting for my husband when this guy..."

"Ma'am, please let me help you."

"Yes, ma'am."

"What is your name?"

"My name is Carolyn Cox, and my car was stolen. It is a black convertible. I am unsure of the license plate number, because I just bought the car. I can tell you how the guy looked who took it."

"I understand. Please describe the perpetrator, and I will put out an APB on him to try to get your vehicle back."

"Absolutely."

I mustered up the best frightened portrayal I could phony up. The dispatcher asked me questions, and I answered them hysterically. I tried to sound as genuine as I could. If the cops stopped him, they would delay him long enough for me to get to his hotel before he made it there.

Sean was completely legit. He never committed a crime in his life. They would have to let him go. All Sean had to do was remain calm and show them his rental papers. At most, getting stopped would be an inconvenience."

"Ma'am, please describe the man who took the car."

"Umm, he had on a mask. The mask was black, like the ones they wear in Aspen where our winter cottage is. He was about six feet tall, and he looked very muscular. I can tell he was a black man, because I could see his skin color underneath his mask."

"Okay, ma'am, I got it. Did the man have any distinguishing marks? Any tattoos, cuts or scars?"

I had to think carefully about my answer. I didn't want my baby to get convicted. I gave her a vague answer. One only a psychologist could decipher.

"It was so dark in the garage. I am unsure. Maybe he did, maybe he didn't. I really don't see many colored folks where I live. Do colored people wear lots of tattoos?"

"Ma'am, I am unsure about that."

"Please just find my car. It is worth over eighty thousand dollars."

"Yes, ma'am, we will get right on it."

Chapter 13
The Hotel

I pulled into hotel's atrium. The valet attendant signaled towards me and offered to park my black beauty for me, but I refused. The self-park lot would work just fine. I was happy enough about not having to shell out twenty bucks a day for in and out privileges. Downtown parking in Chicago was a bad joke. There were never any available parking spots downtown. People were considered lucky if they found a space that was within a one mile of where they were trying to go, let alone a free space in walking distance.

I got out of my rental and locked the doors. I made note of my parking location and walked towards the elevator. I would be damned if I missed the picnic and softball trying to find my damn car. I made it to the elevator and depressed the round white button. The elevator came in no time. I pressed the lobby key on the panel and thought I was on my way. The button lit up.

I looked down to the elevator floorboard. I was tired from the ordeal with the police. I massaged my head like a man beaten, then removed my sunglasses, hoping to see a clearer picture of what was ahead. I was in Chicago, and the first of many reunion events was only a few hours away. First up was the alumni softball game. My high school sweetheart Jade would be there. At least I hoped she would be. How did she look? How did she smell? Did she change at all? Did she reach her goals and life long dream of becoming a psychologist?

I wanted to know. Was she was married? Did she have any children? Where did she live? We had unfinished business, and as far as I was concerned, I was single again. The reunion was the perfect opportunity for us to revisit things. Was there anything left? Had too much time passed? Did she still love me? Time was kind to people with good hearts. A beautiful spirit is the liquid that waters life.

Jade and I certainly needed to talk. Our last moments together were worth forgetting. I said some things, then she said some things, and before I knew it, we were no longer a couple. Even in college, we stayed away from one another. I guess we were both too stubborn to budge. Neither one of us wanted to give the other person an advantage. We lost so much time because of our immovable strength of character.

Then the elevator stopped suddenly. In fact, it jerked. The alarm sounded, and an electronic voice spoke through the overhead speaker.

"Attention Hotel Guest... Attention Hotel Guest...This is the emergency response system. Do not be alarmed. There has been a malfunction to the elevator that should be corrected shortly. Guest Services has been contacted, and they will be dispatched shortly. Please access the red emergency phone located underneath the key panel and use it to contact the front desk by dialing extension 011."

I looked in puzzlement and began to panic. I hated being confined to small spaces, and I certainly didn't want to be suspended three stories in the air stuck in an elevator. I should've taken the stairs!

The voice in the speakers was beginning to annoy me. How was I stuck in an elevator? I did as I was instructed and reached down to pick up the red phone. I dialed extension 011 and a male voice answered. The man sounded overworked and aged.

"Dis is Roscoe in maintenance; how can I help you?"

Why did it seem like all of janitors were named Roscoe, Cleedus or Skip? Why would their parents do that to them?

I spoke loudly into the handset

"Hello., sir, can you hear me?"

"Who dis' on the phone?"

"Mr. Roscoe, can you hear me?"

"I'm tired of y'all kids playin' on that elevator. I'm gonna' come up there and kick y'alls ass!"

This wasn't a false alarm though. I really needed someone to rescue my ass.

"Uh, Roscoe, my name is Sean. I am staying at this hotel. I'm stuck in the elevator. I don't know what happened, but all of a sudden, it just stopped."

"Is that you Rodney, cuz if it is, I'm gonna come down there and hand you an ass whoopin'? Y'all kids gotta learn to stop messin' wit people when they are on their job."

"Mr. Roscoe, this isn't a joke; I am serious. I really am stuck in the elevator. Don't you have a surveillance camera or something that you can use to see who's actually inside of the elevator?"

"Yeah, I've got an elevator for yo' ass! Rodney, I am gonna come down there right now. I've been baking up an ass whooping for you ever since you threw them damn eggs at my Cadillac. I'm coming down there right now. Just you wait!"

"Roscoe? Mr. Roscoe? Hello?"

I stood there stunned. It was hot, and I was baking like a casserole. Only in Chicago. All of a sudden, my phone rang.

Who could this be?

"Hello."

At first, there was silence.

"Hello!" I said again only in a more disquieted tone. I was already hot from the whole elevator thing.

"What are you doing, Sean?'

The tone of voice on the other end of the phone came from a female.

"Who is this?"

"So you've been chattin' it up with so many chickenheads that you can't even recognize your girlfriend's voice anymore. I see now that I can't let you go anywhere by yourself! Do I need to fly down there?"

"Eva, is that you?"

"You're damn right it's Eva! Who the fuck else would it be?"

I took a deep breath. Slid my back down the wall of the elevator and sat down on the floor. I was about to explode. I was hotter than chili peppers in hell. I was in no mood to be hearing shit from my ex-girlfriend.

"Sean, if I would have known you were going to act a damn fool in Chicago, I would have never let you go. I should get on the computer now and look for a one-way ticket."

"Eva, you really need to shut the hell up. Now is not the time. And why are you calling yourself my girlfriend? We are no longer an item."

"Sean, you need to bring your ass back home to Dallas."

I was sweating bullets. Eva had the audacity to call me while I was on vacation and talk to me as if I was a child. Eva was going to get a piece of my mind. She was out of line. I took a deep breath and opened my mouth, but just as I was about to let the words out, my call dropped. I looked down at my cell phone screen. My phone ran out of battery life. I tried powering it on again, but could not get it to stay on. I was livid.

I was on fire! I sat there in that elevator for more than thirty minutes. I finally heard a voice.

"Hello! Hello! Anyone down there? Someone called me and said that they were stuck in the elevator!"

I heard a voice that sounded just like the one I spoke to on the emergency phone.

"Hey! Hey! I'm down here! My name is Sean Jiles and I am the one that called. Help me outta here!"

"Okay, mister, we'll be right down! One of our fuse boxes had a short in it. I am gonna flip a switch and get you going right away, sir. Give me two minutes.

The serviceman left the scene and just like he promised, within two minutes the elevator began moving again. I took the elevator all the way to the lobby. When the doors opened I was accosted by the hotel management staff.

"Mr. Jiles...Mr. Jiles right this way "Mr. Jiles...Mr. Jiles right this way I am the hotel manager. I am so sorry you were stuck in our elevator for so long. This never happens. I want to apologize for your inconvenience. Are you okay?"

"I am alright."

"Can you spare a moment? I would like to have our medical staff take a quick look at you to make sure you are okay..."

John R. Williams

"Lady, no disrespect, but I don't want to see doctor. I've had a long, emotional ass afternoon. I'm okay; I'm cool. I just want to go to my room. I need to get a little rest before my engagement."

"Mr. Jiles, I understand. We feel bad about your experience with the hotel thus far. For your inconvenience, we would like to waive all of your charges for the weekend and upgrade you to a Penthouse Master Suite for the remainder of your stay. It is the least that we can do for all of your troubles."

She had my attention. After saying *"free,"* I was all ears. I was at a four-star hotel. The least expensive room was three hundred dollars per night. I never stayed in a Penthouse Suite before. Even though I wasn't really emotionally distressed, I had to put it on. I had to appear to be discombobulated from the whole elevator experience.

" Now that you've said something, I am feeling a little bit dizzy and dehydrated."

"Mr. Jiles, I completely understand. No worries, I will escort you to your new suite and call room service on your behalf. You can order whatever you like. It's on the house."

Apparently my performance worked.

"Right this way, Mr. Jiles. We will use the Master Suite elevators to get up to your new room."

"Ma'am, wait, I've got to get my things. "

"Oh no, sir, please allow us. The manager instructed the bellhop to gather my belongings and transfer them to the Penthouse Suite."

I followed the manager to a special golden elevator that read *Penthouse Suites*. We got onto the elevator and flew up dozens

96

of floors to the penthouse level. I joked with her about getting stuck again. I said that only this time I'd have company. She joked back by telling me that she'd love to get stuck anywhere with me, because she thought I was handsome. I was flattered.

We got off the elevator. The room she escorted me to was very close to the elevator. I took in the décor. I looked up to the ceiling and saw that it was shaped like an oculus. The walls were covered with fine paintings, and the best paints. The floors were polished white marble. At each corner of the hallway, there were sculptures of angelic figurines. The floors were covered with long Egyptian rugs that had red with gold accents on them.

The whole place oozed sexiness. The seductive furnishings put me in the mood. I could not help but glance at the hotel manager's tight little ass as she switched it from left to right walking through the foyer.

"Mr. Jiles, here are your key cards. Please enjoy the rest of your stay."

"Thank you," I said to the cute authority figure.

"No, thank you," she returned.

I stepped foot inside the palatial space and was simply astounded. The room was definitely more than an upgrade. It was quite striking. It was more than four times the size of the room I had before. It came complete with a fully stocked wet bar, a Jacuzzi tub, terrace style balcony, two extra bedrooms, and the biggest plasma screen I have ever seen at more than fifty-five inches.

I switched on the tube then walked over to the wet bar and made myself a drink. I sipped aged Brandy overlooking the Magnificent Mile. I could see all of the Chicago skyscrapers that made up the skyline. They were all eye level to my room. I could see the Chicago River and the ferryboats treading its pale green waters. I saw the John Hancock building and the Water tower from the balcony.

I glanced down at my watch and hopped up in a panic, I was about to be late. I had to get to the park before I missed the picnic! I ran back inside and took my cell phone out of my pocket. I placed it on its charger and rushed over to my luggage to retrieve my gear. I needed to hustle, if I didn't want to miss playing softball. Most importantly, I did not want to miss seeing Jade.

I took all of my baseball gear out of my suitcase and spread it out on the table. I took off my clothes and hopped into the shower. The five-jet walk-in system was heavenly. I lathered up my towel and began scrubbing my body. In the faint distance, I heard what sounded like a telephone ringing. I was soaking wet and refused to step out of the shower. I just knew it couldn't have been my cell phone, because I had it powered off. I ignored it. I finished cleaning my body and exited the shower. I rubbed on some deodorant, tossed on some cologne, and used baby oil to grease up my skin. I exited the bathroom, went back into the master bedroom, and threw on my gear. I looked like the general manager of a professional team with my edged up goatee and fitted cap. I grabbed my wallet and car keys then headed towards the door. On my way out the door, I noticed a red flashing light on the telephone system indicating that I had a voice message on the hotel phone. *I guess it was ringing while I was in the shower.* I started to go back into the room and check the message to see who had called, but I chose not to. I was in a hurry.

I walked out the door and down the hall to the special elevator. I hit the elevator button and patted my jogging pants pockets down to see if I had my cell phone. I did not have it. I started to do a u-turn and double back to see if I had left it in the room but decided against it. The elevator came. I hopped in and took it down to the basement level where the garage connection was. I made it to the garage and then hit the panic alarm on my keychain to sound the sedan horn; I could not remember where I parked. As the horn blasted in tempo and echoed against the concrete beams, I found the car in no time. I hopped in, cranked up my sound system, and sped out of the hotel garage. I hit the freeway and did sixty miles an hour all the way to my exit on 55th Street, otherwise known as the Low End.

Ten years ago, the Low End of town had undergone a transformation. The same two- and three-flat Brownstone buildings that were once condemned and filled with crack heads were now multi-million dollar mansions. The raggedy apartment buildings that were once low-income housing were now lavish condominiums for the city's elite. It seemed that investors and professionals were finally appreciating what so many appreciated back then, its character. It was nauseating seeing yuppies walking around with their briefcases and tiny dogs, smiling and laughing, as if they had a true connection with urban living. They were all thrilled about parking their luxury exotics in front of their homes as if they had lived in the hood forever. They were now leaving their doors unlocked in the same neighborhood that they were afraid to drive through just ten years ago.

I remembered walking past those same buildings as a kid. I grew up four blocks away from where I was headed. I coasted past the same corner stores and gas stations my grandparents played numbers at. For almost twenty years, my grandparents played their favorite numbers to no avail, throwing away thousands of dollars until one day the numbers hit, and they actually won. My grandparents won the Big Pot Jackpot and walked away with more than seven hundred thousand dollars.

When they received the money, the first thing they bought were a matching set of shiny new Cadillac's and a flashy new designer wardrobe. They paid off their bills, and then used the remainder of the winnings to purchase two refurbished, six-unit, three flat buildings. Each building was marvelous; they both had over ten thousand square feet of space. Instead of immediately finding renters and turning profits on the properties, they decided to bless family members with a place to live for one year at no charge. The aim was to help struggling family members get on their feet. Instead, my kinfolk let the streets snatch them. They all used the extra money they saved on rent to buy drugs and alcohol. They ran the streets and did just about anything to score their next hit, everyone except for my mother.

My mother was a hard worker. She refused to take her parents' handouts. She and Daddy were very proud souls. They worked hard for everything they had. The only thing they didn't have was a place to call home. They saved down payment money for years, but never had enough. When my grandparents saw how hard their youngest daughter worked, they decided to help. Enough was enough. My grandparents kicked every single one of their kids out of the building and sold it to the first bidder that came along. They gave a portion of the money to my mom and dad to get their first home. The six-unit building sold for more than six-hundred thousand dollars. That was a hell of a lot of money in the early eighties. Now that same building listed for two million dollars. It was surreal.

I saw the entrance to Washington Park. I could see the signage and crowded parking lots. I rolled my windows up and closed the sunroof. I couldn't wait to see my friends. While looking for a spot, I noticed a compact sized car tailgating my car. Apparently, the driver had astigmatism. They were about two inches away from crashing into my rear fender. I could not make out the driver, but I could tell it was a woman. The driver was dangerously close, so I took a sharp left onto a residential street and looked for the first parking space I could find. There were none in sight, but I had lost my hatchback

I checked my rearview mirror again and was relieved to see that my tailgater was no longer behind me. I drove around the block and located a space decent enough to park my rental. It was near the alleyway. I drove up next to the space and began the proverbial parallel park routine. I placed my left hand in the ten o'clock position, and my right hand on the back of my passenger's seat. I turned my head to make sure the space was big enough to fit my car. The spot was just fine but was my car safe. I was on the edge of the alleyway and could see all the way to the next block, I looked further down the alleyway and couldn't believe my eyes. At the end of the block was the red compact car from earlier. What was really going on? .

Chapter 14
Home Sweet Home

I enjoyed the blanket of the sun while strolling down North Clark Street. Every time I flew into Chicago, I made time to stop in my favorite café, Chloe's. The café was a well-known greasy spoon on Clark Street near the University. Chloe's was a Creole inspired eatery that had unmistakable charm. The owner, whose name was actually Chloe, was a doll. Over the years, I became a regular. Chloe knew about my dreams of making it big and touching the world through my writing. Over time, we grew close. We e-mailed each other from time to time, and when she decided to market the café, I helped her create a web site, and even did a little side promotion for her by hosting meetings and think tanks for writers there.

Chloe's gained its stardom in a paradoxical way. One December afternoon, a film producer, on the brink of insanity, stopped into the café for brunch. He wisely decided to take time out of his day and break away from set to collect his thoughts. Bad acting and budgetary constraints made him contemplate abandoning his project, but he changed his mind after having a meal at Chloe's.

Chloe saw the troubled man in her café and felt sorry for him. She didn't know who he was or why he was so flustered. He was unshaven and seemed like the type that always had a million things on his mind. Being a true saint, she offered him a free cup of coffee and a pastry. To her, the act of compassion was small potatoes. It didn't cost her a thing, and she knew it would cheer him up. She had no idea that her Samaritan act would make his day.

Chloe brewed him a cup of her signature blend coffee. It was Chloe's very own java recipe. She made it with cinnamon, nutmeg, and fresh vanilla bean shavings. It was the perfect mix of bold and smooth. She delivered the steaming hot coffee to the director and then invited him to sit in the plush Quiet Zone area of the building. It was a special area within the café that had to be reserved for personal use. The room had soundproof doors and windows. The room was perfect for the director. The director indulged in the solitude, and except for getting up to get slices of pecan pie, he stayed in the Quiet Zone room for the better part of that afternoon. He immediately fell in love with Chloe's.

The director had connections in Hollywood. He loved Chloe's so much that he put Chloe's Café on an unspoken A-list of preferred vendors for movie shoots. Chloe's quickly became an underground success. The café was featured in over a dozen Indie films. Now celebrities, locals, and neighborhood artists rush into her place for a cup of java. Not only has business quadrupled, the café has kept its charm.

I drew nearer to the entrance and noticed that Chloe had given the front façade of the building a facelift. The building exterior looked like it belonged on Bourbon Street in old New Orleans. The building mimicked a saltbox house complete with a gallery roof and large white colony pillars extending from the sidewalk to the uppermost point of the edifice. Chloe installed a cast-iron wrap.

As I stared up from street level, I envisioned patrons enjoying French Roast, thinking up the next big idea. I unzipped my jacket and walked through the entrance doors. Upon entering, I took a whiff of the aromas permeating the air. I smelled coffee beans, tealeaves, and baked goods. I scoured the room looking for Chloe but did not see her.

I walked to the counter and looked at the menu. I always ordered the same items every time I went to the café. It was refreshing to see the variety that was available to me, but I stuck with the same combination every time. I fixed my mouth to order my usual when all of a sudden Chloe walked to the front area.

Chloe was easy to spot. She had electric red hair and always wore eccentric eyeglasses that were sophisticated and flashy. She was the type of woman that could walk into any room, anywhere, and everyone would notice her. Despite the fact that she was at least sixty years old, Father Time had treated her well. She had few wrinkles, and her figure still had shape to it. Aside from her worn hands, she could have easily passed for forty-five. I hollered out to her like an excited kid.

"Hey there, pretty girl! I see that the sunshine is still out this afternoon. It's mighty fine bumping into you again."

"Well look at what the cat drug in. Mr. Phenomenal himself; right here among us in the flesh, come over her and give me a hug, boy!"

I ran over to Chloe and hugged her. Onlookers were confused by our weird name-calling. Instead of using our legal names, we used nicknames. "Sean, I hope you brought some copies of that new book. The kids have been talking about it since it was released. I love the title too, *The Day My Life Was No More;* it's the perfect title for your book!"

"I brought some. You had better put a copy in your front window with the others."

"I will."

The server at the counter smiled and asked Chloe if I was her son. I cleverly retorted and told the young woman that Chloe was my fiancée. Chloe giggled.

"Boy, stop! Sweetheart this is Sean Jiles. He is an author and one of my very first customers. We gave each other those nicknames one summer after he helped me catch a mugger that tried to rob my café."

I remembered the story like it happened yesterday.

It was Fourth of July weekend, and I was at Chloe's café late that evening. I passed on the downtown festivals and focused on my writing. Every weekend I spent hours in the Quiet Zone jolted from caffeine. Even back then, I spent time perfecting lines and getting words to fit together right.

Like clockwork, every evening before closing, Chloe signaled to me letting me know that it was closing time. She used a two-fingered signal and gave me my clue to pack it up. As much as she liked me, she always had long days in the café. When it was quitting time, Chloe bounced out of that place like a basketball.

I packed my things and began to head out when without warning, a loud crash echoed. It sounded like shattered glass. The sound ricocheted off the walls. It was too loud to ignore.

I looked to the front of the store and saw Chloe being held at gunpoint by a masked vagrant. He had Chloe in a chokehold.

Even though his back was facing me, I could hear Chloe begging for mercy. The masked man spoke to her.

"Hey, pretty lady... I don't want no trouble! All I want is the money."

"Oh my God, please let me go."

"Shut up, bitch! Hurry up and gimme the money. I need to get me a fix!"

"Pleas, sir, I'll give you anything you want, just don't hurt me."

My heart pounded through my chest. My palms began to get sweaty and my heart rate tripled. My breathing grew heavy, and I was riddled with fear. I hid behind the condiments station, trying to remain silent and still.

"Don't make me hurt you, bitch! Is that what you want? I need that fucking money, and I ain't leaving until I get it!"

"Sir, I will cooperate with you. I will give you all the cash I have. Just don't hurt me, please. I have a family."

Chloe tried to reason with the vagrant, but it was useless. He did not listen to reason. If no one stepped in, Chloe could get hurt. I swallowed my fear, composed myself, and made a choice to help her. I looked for any weapon in sight. I spotted one. I quietly inched over to a nearby table that was hidden from plain view. I grabbed a mini-skillet that was left on a table. It still had the remnants of leftover cinnamon rolls in it. I kneeled back down and crept closer towards the vagabond. Using the reflection from chrome accented espresso machines; I looked to the front of the store and made sure that Chloe was still okay. The robber yelled at her once again. Chloe started crying. She completely lost her composure.

The Reunion

"Take me to the money, bitch! I need that cash right now!"

"Right this way, sir."

Chloe pointed to the register and began taking baby steps towards it. I didn't know if she saw me hiding behind that shelf or if it was the mercy of God, but she lead him right towards me. Still afraid, I took a deep breath and said a silent prayer for strength. I asked God for enough strength to knock the robber out with my skillet.

Chloe walked closer, her mugger close behind. I rose up from behind the shelving unit and crowned the man senseless. I swung the skillet as hard as I could and connected with the man's head. The robber was knocked out cold. He fell to the floor and rested flat on his face. Blood oozed slowly out of the gash on the back of his head where I hit him. The impact ejected the gun from his grasp. Chloe picked up the gun and pointed it at the man. She began thanking God for her safety.

I was a nervous wreck. I couldn't believe the events that took place. We could have both died that evening.

"Are you okay, Sean?"

"Yes, I'm fine. Are you okay, Ms. Chloe?"

"I'm okay, sweetheart. Thank God you were here. I don't know what I would have done had I been here by myself. Please grab the phone and call 9-1-1."

"That's a good idea, Ms. Chloe."

The authorities arrived. Chloe told the authorities every detail of the break-in. I sat down and sipped the remnants of my cold coffee."

Chloe finished up with the police. Chloe came back over to the seating area to talk to me.

"I need a drink, Sean. Do Ms. Chloe a favor and reach behind the coffee bar and grab that bottle of liquor for me."

I did as instructed and reached behind the counter to grab the bottle. Before I passed it to her, I opened the top and smelled the strong alcohol. I had never taken a drink in my life. I didn't know the difference between brandy, ripple or scotch. Chloe pulled two glasses down from the top cabinet behind the counter.

"What a night; we need a drink."

"We?" I said.

"Yes, *we*; don't play crazy. Pour us a couple of drinks."

" Okay then."

Although I had never taken in liquor before that night, Chloe and I drank good whiskey and let it melt away our uneasiness. My teenage belly burned from the sting of good brown. I started to feel a rumbling sound in my stomach. I vomited all over the floor. It looked disgusting. Embarrassed, I sopped up the barf with a napkin and threw it away. Chloe laughed.

"Sean, are you okay?"

"I'm fine. I don't know what happened, I just…"

"Don't worry about it. I want to let you know that I really appreciate what you did tonight took courage. I'm glad you helped me."

"You're welcome. I just didn't want anything to happen to you. I wouldn't have been able to live with myself if you got hurt. My father used to say that in man's darkest hour he must find blind courage."

"Your father sounds like a wise man."

"He was a wise man. He passed away some years ago."

"I'm sorry."

"It's okay, Ms. Chloe; that was a long time ago."

"Well, Sean, your father would have been proud of you tonight."

"Thanks, Ms. Chloe."

"Sean, stop all of that 'Ms. Chloe' stuff. You are family now. We need nicknames."

"Okay, how about pretty lady?"

"Why that name?"

"The guy who tried to mug you called you pretty lady. I can't believe he used flattery and tried to rob you."

"You do make a good point, Sean. I must admit that I do like the sound of it. So be it. Now you need a nickname."

"Ms. Chloe, I mean, pretty lady, that's not necessary."

"Oh yes it is; it'll be our own special thing, our own little secret. You've earned a nickname. Hmmm…let me see. I know! I've got it! I will call you Mr. Phenomenal! Yes! That's perfect! Mr. Phenomenal will be your new nickname!"

I looked at her with crossed eyes, half drunk from the good dranky-drank.

"Why that name?"

I was genuinely puzzled as to why she chose such a magical name. It sounded sensational; kind of like a superhero or something. I didn't deserve that.

"Well, Sean, you may not think so, but what you did today was phenomenal. This coffee shop is all I that I have. You helped save my livelihood. You helped preserve my dream, and *that* is why you are phenomenal."

"As far as I'm concerned, your money is no good to me now. From this day forward, every time you step foot inside the café, everything is on the house. Drink all the coffee, tea, and espresso you want. It is the least I can do. You now have lifetime freebies."

"Thank you, pretty lady. Are you sure? Do you really want to do that? I can go through a pot of gourmet coffee in no time, I drink coffee like it's water."

"I'm sure you can, but you've earned it."

"Very well, I'm no fool! You have yourself a deal."

I snapped back into reality. That special day was so long ago. I walked back over to the front counter with Chloe beside me. I was about to place my order when she interrupted me mid-sentence.

"I think I'll have..."

"Allow me. He always orders the *same* thing. He'll have the signature coffee with a slice of sweet potato pie."

"Thank you."

The sweet potato pie was a decadent dessert that she baked fresh every few hours. It was that popular. The cashier spoke to me again.

"Okay, so you are having a signature coffee and a slice of sweet potato pie, correct?"

She quoted a price. I reached for my wallet, but Chloe snatched my wallet away from me.

"Sean, you're gonna hurt an old woman's feelings. Your order is on me."

"You don't have to do that; I'm gonna pay this time."

"No, you aren't. You're not gonna make me out to be a liar. I've already told you that your money was no good in here."

The cashier closed the register and zeroed out the balance. She handed me my items. I could not wait to dig in. Chloe took me upstairs to the Quiet Zone area. Once there we caught up on lost time.

"So, what's been going on in your neck of the woods?"

"I've stayed busy. My family is fine, and the writing is coming along."

"That's great to hear! I love to see black men doing positive things in the community and for themselves. So many young brothers are caught up in the system, trying to get that fast money. Instead of getting jobs and roughing through those tough times, they do otherwise."

"I know what you mean. I know people like that. They are as sharp as tacks but can't stay out of trouble."

"I heard some students in the 'café a while back talking about how you won some kind of award or something?"

"Oh yeah, I forgot to mention it to you."

"What happened?"

"I won a grant. I was given one hundred thousand dollars to produce my first stage play."

"Really?"

"Yup, I got the check in the mail last week."

"Well bless His name! That is great news, Sean."

"You can say that again. That was the main reason I stopped by to see you. I wanted to share the good news with you in person."

"What will the play be about?"

"I don't want to spoil it for you, but the whole premise is about finding lost love. The play is focused on a man who goes back home to his ten year class reunion in search of love. The main character's name is John."

111

"Oh really, Sean, I guess that was a real stretch. Please tell me that you are not going to air out your dirty laundry with this play, are you?"

"No way. You know me better than that. I am going to keep it classy."

"Tell me more."

"The main character was modeled after me. We have the same passions and the same dreams. The play has a pretty powerful theme."

"Really?"

"Yes. The theme is love and change. Face it, people change. Sometimes the change is for good and other times it is for the bad. All you need to do is factor in time, stress, and circumstance, and just about anybody is capable of doing anything."

"You are right about that."

"I want to put on a play that will change the way people feel about love and life."

"It sounds like you are well on your way. Work must be going great."

"Well, pretty lady, to be honest with you it couldn't be going any better. I think the main reason is because I don't think of what I do as work. I was given the chance to live out my dreams, and that's very rare nowadays."

"Yes it is."

"I've been working on the project for three years. It's the manuscript I was meant to write. I really believe that it will be the definitive work that will put me on the map."

"I am so happy for you, Sean. That is awesome. I knew that someday someone out there would recognize your talents and give you your big break."

"Thanks for all of the support you have given me over the years. Your coffee shop has always been like a second home to me. Anytime I needed to work on material, I knew I could find peace in your coffee shop. I love this place."

"That means a lot to me, Sean."

"Whatever, I'm just an average guy and--"

"Now you stop that kind of talk, Sean! Listen to me, God has given you a gift. You have the chance to reach millions of people with your writing. Hold your head up and be proud. Remember that."

"Yes, ma'am."

We sat there chatting about her business and ideas for the play. I felt completely comfortable with her. I admired her strength and her essence. She was the epitome of a woman. I respected her opinions and her conclusions; she was a success story .She came from the bottom and rose to the top. She could actually get through to me.

"Okay, Sean, on to the next topic. What's going on with that fiery girlfriend of yours? You know I never did like her, not even a little bitch, oops, I meant little bit."

"Hey now, pretty lady, stop that; don't call her names."

"Sean, she is not a good fit for you. I remember how she used to interrupt you when we spoke on the phone, and question your judgment and accuse you of sleeping around. One time I even heard her pouting about not showing her enough attention."

"Was it that bad?"

"I'm sorry, Sean, but yes. Deep down you know it to be true. That girl has been a handful ever since you hooked up with her.

I hated to admit it, but Chloe did have a point.

"Sean, all I am trying to say is that the type of woman a man chooses to have at his side says a lot about him. You *must* choose carefully."

"I understand what you are saying. Eva and I broke up a couple of days ago."

"Hallelujah!"

"You are a mess," I said playfully.

Chloe was correct; a woman could be a man's gift or his curse. Imagine how different the world would be if Adam never ate from the Tree of Life. Better yet, imagine if Eve never gave Adam the fruit in the first place.

"Sean, hear me when I tell you this. *Everyone* has a choice, and we choose our own way. The question is, are you happy now?"

I paused for a moment. The silence was thick and uncomfortable. I did not know how to respond. I was finally free, but I longed for the companionship of a partner.

"I am happy, but…"

"Nope, shut your mouth. It took you too long to answer. You aren't happy, but I do see a certain twinkle of hope in your eyes. Let's change the subject again."

Chloe warmed the moment back up with her warm smile and another piping hot cup of coffee. I knew she didn't mean any harm with her comments. She simply wanted to provoke my thoughts like she had done so many times before. She succeeded.

"It's okay, pretty lady; I appreciate the feedback."

"Sean, I apologize. I need to get some business of my own instead of worrying about yours. You know I love you, boy. You are the son I never had."

Chloe's words resonated deep within my soul. Over the years, I ran from the truth. It was easy creating characters and weaving outcomes through my work, but it was uncomfortable talking about it. For nearly ten years, I wrote about the challenges of finding true love, and now I faced them myself."

"I feel you, pretty lady. I just need time to think things through. I don't want to make a brash decision and regret it later. "

"I understand. I will leave it alone."

I sighed in relief.

"So what else do you want to talk about? I have to get going in a moment. I have a picnic to go to?"

"Is that why you're in town? You never told me why you flew up here."

"This weekend is my ten year high school class reunion. We are having a picnic, a banquet, and even a happy hour. That's why I flew in."

"Sounds like fun."

"It should be. Lord knows I need to have some fun."

"So, whatever happened to that nice chocolate girl I used to see you with all the time when you lived in Chicago? She seemed like such a nice girl."

"Who do you mean?"

I knew exactly whom she was referring.

Please don't act funny; you know who I'm talking about. You know that chocolate-colored girl that I used to see you with a long time ago. I think you told me once that you two went to high school together or something like that. She was *really* pretty, and you two looked so cute together."

"Oh, I know who you are talking about now. Her name was... well, her name is Jade. She is okay. We haven't talked to each other in a long time. Our last conversation was four or five years ago, and it wasn't a good one. We had a fight."

"What were you two fighting about?"

Chloe started to pry.

"Well, she didn't think I loved her as much as I did. I didn't think she trusted me as much as she did. We were both so young and so naïve back then. What we didn't understand was that we both cared about each other very deeply. We were fighting the same fight. It doesn't matter now though."

"Sean, you two seemed like a match made in heaven. When you came in here, y'all looked so happy together. Y'all both had that beautiful brown skin. You two looked like African royalty standing next to one another. It seemed like all was right with the world. She was so nice and smart too. You can tell that her mother and father raised her up right with some good home training. I really liked her. That was always the type of woman I saw you settling down with."

"So in addition to being a coffee shop owner, you're a match-maker too."

"Come on, Sean. You can't look me straight in the eye and tell me that you don't still care about her."

"That was a long time ago. That chapter of my life was left unwritten."

"Then rewrite it, Sean. Something might still be there."

"Listen to me, that situation is done, over, caput, finished."

"Why are you getting defensive? That's how I know you still care for her."

Chloe cut deep. I thought about Jade every day for the past six years. She was my first *real* true love, and I let her slip away.

I was never able to stomach that fact. I should have fought for her. Our relationship shattered into a million little pieces, and we didn't try hard enough to reassemble the mosaic. We just quit.

Chloe went back to the kitchen to get a refill for our empty cups. She also retrieved the last slice of sweet potato pie and served it to me. I finished the last morsels of my pie and packed up my things. I left her a dozen copies of my book then put on my jacket. I gave Chloe a bear hug and a kiss on the cheek then started on my goodbyes.

"Well, pretty lady, I have to go. I have that picnic to go to, dinner with my mom, and a bunch of other class reunion events, so I have to get going."

"I understand. If you've gotta go, then you've gotta go. It was so nice to see you again. Don't be a stranger."

"I won't. Take care."

I walked towards the exit. Just before I could step foot outside, Chloe asked me one final question.

"Do you still love her?"

Chapter 15
The Picnic

I parked my rental close to the curb and exited my car. Maybe I was paranoid for no reason. I dismissed all negative notions and remembered the reason why I was at the park in the first place--the picnic.

I wasn't myself, I had to shake off the bullshit and transform into the confident, fun-loving Sean that people remembered. I had to become organized before I reconnected with my classmates. After all, I had a lot to be grateful for. Eva's nagging ass was eight hundred miles away in Texas; I had a Penthouse Suite at a four-star hotel in the middle of the city, and a pocket full of cash. Not to mention I still had my youth and good looks. I settled down quickly.

I looked to my left and saw more than a hundred people laughing, eating, and congregating near the baseball diamond. Washington Park was the perfect place to host our reunion picnic. It was large enough to accommodate my graduating class and was the most picturesque park available via the Chicago Park District.

I depressed my car alarm and walked towards my fellow alums. I strolled across the grassy patches of grass. I looked down at my shoes and outfit. I gave myself a quick once over to make sure I looked presentable. I looked great. As I walked past the front entrance of the park, I took a quick sniff of my underarms and proceeded. Nothing was worse than smelling like a wildebeest. People always remember a man that smells good, and never forget a man that smells bad.

"What's up, Sean?" A male voice yelled out my name like they were high on life.

There was only one person on earth that loud. He sounded like a sixteen-year-old groupie at a rock concert. It was Miles White. Miles was a six foot three, two-hundred fifty pound block of country bumpkin that played football for Kensor High back in the day. He was an All-American that everybody loved for his athletic ability. He was from Chicago, but spoke with an accent that sounded like the South. He was the truth back in the day. He played middle linebacker and in his senior year, held the single-season sack record. I used to watch him ravage opposing teams like a madman. He could figure out a snap count faster than anyone in football. People thought he was a psychic with extrasensory abilities, because it seemed like every down he planted people in the dirt.

"I know I'm in Chicago now! What's up, Miles?"

I went over to my friend and gave him a hug.

He laughed. "Sean Jiles! What's good wit cha? I see you still have that big peanut head. You look like Nestle Snipes."

His comical greeting wasn't insulting; he was simply letting me know that he missed a brother.

"I know you aren't talking shit, big boy. You big soy sauce spittin, biscuit eatin, hungry jack wanna be. Man, what's up with you, dawg? I haven't heard from you in a while. How have you been?"

My equally insulting comeback made him smile, which was hard to do for a man so menacing on the surface.

"I've been maintaining, man. Everything is copasetic."

"Oooh, copasetic, I see somebody decided to go to college after graduation."

"I see you are still the silliest cat in the world. I heard about the book and the play. Congratulations. I better get in good with you now before you blow up and start actin' funny towards me."

I chuckled. Miles was a true nutcase, but he did have a point. It seemed like every time someone from the hood got on, they pulled a switcheroo and conveniently forgot where they came from. Somehow having money and designer labels made them forgot what a good piece of fried chicken or cornbread tasted like.

"Now you are gonna stop with that, man. I am still the same dude. I grew up a few blocks from here. I ain't changed one bit, fat ass. I am still the same ol' Sean!"

"Uh huh, tell me anything. On the real, I read your novel, and I must admit, your material is tight! You are gonna shock the world someday."

"Thanks. Where's the food?"

"I think the eats are over there, by your girl." He snickered.

"Oh shit...here we go again. By my girl, huh? Who's my girl supposed to be?"

"Don't play crazy, Sean; you know who I am talking about. Look to your right, she's sitting over there by the grill."

I refocused my retinas. I had only dealt with a few chicks back in the day, and all of them were easy on the eyes. The only woman

I saw in the distant horizon resembled a female bodybuilder. She had to weigh at least two hundred fifty pounds.

"Miles, I know you aren't talking about who I think you are talking about, are you?"

"Oh hell yeah. Go on over there and give your baby a big ol' sloppy kiss."

Miles was referring to Keisha Brown, the only girl in our graduating class who could outright stomp the shit out of any man. If there had been a female prison gang in high school, she would have been the leader. She was a bad chick. What made it so bad was that she was actually a cutie pie. It's just that she was built like a wrestler.

She had huge arms and thunder thighs. She had unusually large titties that had to be at least a size double D. All of the boys in school made jokes. They even gave her a nickname. They used to call her Soccer Ball. Even though she wore bras all the time, one could still see her nipples through her clothes. Her dark brown areolas made imprints through her attire. It was as if she was aroused all the time. People made legitimate passes at her, but she always took offense. Poor thing. She never had boyfriends throughout high school.

Keisha and I had a great friendship. She took quite a liking to me. Unlike the other guys, I never made childish remarks to her. We rode the same bus after school and spent hours on end discussing music, fashion, and sports. I cared about her, but never enough to feel for her the way she felt for me.

In our sophomore year, we were both selected to participate in the school fundraiser. Each year the principle hosted a carnival to raise funds for the school. We invited clowns, had carnival themed games, and the ever-popular dunk tank. For two dollars, students were given five softballs and a chance to sink a fellow student in the icy cold water. Keisha and I drew the small straws and had to be guinea pigs. All of the girls took a crack at sinking me, and the boys at Keisha.

I went an entire day bone dry. I was untouched; none of the girls were skillful enough to sink me. Keisha on the other hand got dunked repeatedly. By the final hour, she had raised almost two hundred dollars by herself. The memory that stuck out most came at the end of her shift. She was about to leave when this one asshole stole one of the softballs and launched it clear across the crowd. The softball hit the bull's eye mark and submerged Keisha in the dunk tank.

She was livid! It caught her completely off guard. She rose up out of the tank screaming expletives. Not only did the boy not pay, he started making jokes. Keisha went into bitch mode.

"You grimy, bastard! I am gonna kick your ass! Just wait until I catch up to you!"

She hopped out of the pool. She was soaking wet. She chased after the jokester at full throttle. I jumped out of the pool and ran after her, because I knew that if she caught hold to him, she would stomp a bone out of his ass. I didn't want her to get expelled. I had to prevent the beat down. I yelled out to her.

"Keisha! Keisha...wait! Don't do it!"

She ran a block and a half at full speed and finally caught up to the boy. She grabbed him and put him into a sleeper hold. The poor boy was almost lifeless. I pleaded with her.

"Keisha, wait, you don't wanna do this."

"Yes, I do, Sean. I'm getting tired of having to take their shit every day. People keep on fuckin' with me. Enough is enough! He is going to pay."

Keisha had a point. She had been teased every day for two straight years. The teenagers at the school were cruel and heartless. They let their hormones get the best of them. They had teased her to the point of insanity. She didn't deserve it, neither did the poor kid. Not by damn sight.

"Keisha, just wait a minute, please…"

"Why, Sean? Huh? Why?"

I had to think quickly. I only knew one way to calm her down and get her off the boy.

"Keisha, listen to me. I want to apologize for him. He's an asshole. What he did was wrong, but he is not worth the time of day. You are so much more than what people see. I think so highly of you, and I don't want to see you make a mistake. You will regret it later. I was hoping that after this whole carnival thing we could go hang out somewhere. Maybe we can grab a bite to eat or get a milkshake at the grill. The air is warm tonight; maybe we could take a walk on the lakefront and talk for a while, just you and me. Just let him go.

"But, Sean, you know how people tease me. It gets on my nerves."

"I ain't gonna lie to you, Keisha. You do have a big chest, but there's more to you than just your breasts. You are a beautiful person too. I like your mind, body, and spirit."

I was as smooth as silk. Keisha began to loosen her grip. The boy was no longer in a chokehold. Keisha let him go and he ran off. Keisha started crying. She fell to the ground, exhausted from the ordeal. I embraced her and comforted her with my words.

"Keisha, it'll be okay. Don't cry. I'm sorry I stepped in, but I don't want to see you ruin your future.

Keisha snuggled with me and stopped crying. She and I were now soaking wet. More than an hour passed since the end of the carnival. We were all alone sitting on a side street sidewalk. I hugged her close and whispered into her ear.

"It's okay now; it's gonna be okay."

She hugged me tighter and tighter, and I could smell her essence from below. She smelled like honey and cinnamon. I lost my focus. Her voluptuous physique pressing against my chest, before we knew it, we were French kissing. No one saw us. For that instant, time stood still. We were completely wrapped in the moment.

Things between us never went past kissing, but what we shared will never be forgotten. It felt good to let myself go and let myself feel. We shared a secret that we never told a soul.

I snapped back into reality. Miles handed me a beer and began teasing me again.

"Sean and Keisha sitting in a tree, K.I.S.S.I.N.G."

"Miles, you are a dumb ass. Leave me alone about that shit. You are just mad because no one wanted to be with your funny looking ass. Your head looks like a sucked dark-chocolate M&M. Why don't you go out and find a city that needs some nighttime and help them out with your dark-skinned ass."

Miles laughed at my comeback. Then he whipped out his cell phone and asked for my cell number.

"All right then, Sean, I have to get outta here, man."

" It was good seeing you again."

"One more thing, Sean, all bullshit aside, you are doing the damn thang with your plays and those books. Make us proud, baby boy. You got a lot of people pulling for you."

I was genuinely touched. His words resonated.

"Thanks a million my midnight colored brother, I gotcha! I will make it do what it do, big pimpin."

"There you go again with the dark-skinned jokes. You of *all* people shouldn't be making fun of anybody's complexion. You and I are the same shade of black wit' ya ink spot ass. Later man, one love."

I twisted the cap off my imported beer and took a long swig. I walked closer towards the commotion. I saw Keisha and the other alums. I walked over to them with the same confident swagger that I had when I was a teen. I could hear subwoofer speakers playing the latest neo-soul cuts. While I didn't know the name of the song playing, I fell in love with the drum pattern and cellos playing in the melody. The song hypnotized all that heard it. People were doing the electric slide and having a great time.

I eased into my surroundings and discovered a newfound cool as I approached Keisha. Her back was turned away from me, so my stealth-like approach startled her.

"Keisha! What's up, girl? Show me some love!"

Keisha turned around and her eyes lit up. Her huge chestnut colored eyes sparkled in the sunlight. She looked well. Her figure was better looking up close than from far away. She had on a pair of khaki colored shorts and an off-white tank top. She had lost weight and even though her brassiere was just as large as it was back in the day, her body looked noticeably different. I tried not to stare, but it was hard.

"Hey, Sean!"

Keisha gave me a bear hug and kissed me on the cheek.

"Oh my God! How have you been? It is so good to see you, Sean. A few of us had a little wager as to whether or not you would actually show up."

"What? Now you know there can't be a class reunion without me. I wouldn't have missed this for the world."

"When did you get in? I heard you were down in the Dirty South; how do you like it?"

"It's beautiful. I touched down earlier today."

"Are you serious?"

" Yes, all they need down there is a Halsted Mall."

"Not the Halsted Mall, no you didn't. You know as well as I do that Halsted Mall clothes look like pimp clothes. All they sell are bright colors. If you would have come here dressed in a pink suit and a cane, I would have screamed."

"Keisha stop...please quit it, you are hurtin' my kidneys."

Keisha had a point. Everyone from Chicago knew about the Halsted Mall. It was a collection of specialty shops that spanned six blocks. Eager shoppers could find gator-boots in any color there. Countless people went there to get their duds. At least twenty people at the prom had on pink alligator shoes. Where on earth do pink alligators live?

"Sean, let's cut to the chase...I have two questions for you."

"Okay. I'm all ears. What do you want to know? I am an open book."

"Question one... am I in any of your books?"

"No. You are *not* in any of my books. I wouldn't even ask you first though. I would just put you in them."

"You are still a cocky son of a bitch, aren't you?"

"You know how I do."

"Whatever, Sean."

"Seriously, you are very special to me, and I would never do that. Usually the characters I create have issues, and they are pretty off track in their lives. You are none of those things."

"Aww, you are gonna make me vomit, Sean. Stop coming at me with that old nineteen ninety-seven script. We aren't at homecoming. Question two... when is the play coming to Chicago?"

"I thought I let the cat out of the bag. I am finishing it up as we speak. I still have to write a few final pages. Once I finish, I start touring. The plan is to start in New York and end up in Chicago for the final stretch."

"Mr. Jiles, you are doing it big. I am so happy for you!"

"Stop that, you know I am still the same dude. I am going to keep it real too. I love my hometown, and I gotta show it love. Sometimes I wish I still lived in Chicago."

"Ain't nothing left for you here, Sean. The city may look different, but it is still the same at its core. Chicago has the same mess. Going away to school was the right choice. Do you remember Jodi?"

"How could I forget? He was a tough dude. He tried to fight me six times when we were in high school. How is he doing?"

"You haven't heard, Sean?"

"Heard what?" I asked in pure conundrum. I knew that Jodi was always up to no good, but he was a survivor. He could have been a four-star general in the armed forces, but he chose to lead a different group of soldiers. His army was in the streets. Keisha spoke again.

"Jodi is dead. He was killed a couple years ago over some dumb shit."

"Really?"

"Yeah, it was all over the news. He stuck up a liquor store and the owner shot him."

"Are you serious? Death ain't nothing to play with. Tell me this is a bad joke or something."

Keisha told me that Jodi began selling drugs. Eventually he started experimenting. Soon thereafter, he was a fiend. One night he and some of his addict friends ran low on cash. They tried pulling a robbery, but things took a turn for the worse. I was shocked. I continued the dialogue.

"So if I am hearing you correctly, Jodi is dead?"

"Yes, he's gone."

I poured out a little liquor in his memory and said a blessing for him in my mind.

"That's why it's so good to see a brother like you living their dream. Despite everything you have accomplished, you are grounded, and you still have a kind heart."

"I am just being me."

"Also, I never got the chance to thank you for what you did for me that day. It meant a lot to me to have at least *one* person that cared and gave a damn. I will always love you for that. I honestly don't know what would have happened if you weren't there."

"Come on now, you are giving me too much credit. I was just being a good friend. You had your whole life ahead of you, and that asshole didn't deserve to be the reason for your demise. He was a piece of shit."

"Yes, he was!"

"You did whoop his ass though, Keisha. You went down in the history books for that one. You choked the shit outta him. You were off tha' chain."

The mood grew prickly. I knew that sooner or later I would have to address why Keisha and I never hooked up. I tried to change the subject by asking another question. Yielding avoidance never hurt anyone. Keisha was a nice girl, but she wasn't my cup of tea, and she knew it. Besides, we were better at being friends.

"What are you up to nowadays?"

"I'm just taking care of my little boy and trying to go back to school and finish up my degree. I took a few semesters off, if you know what I mean."

"You have a little boy? Like as in a child?"

"Yes, I have a child. His name is Travis, and he is the only thing that keeps me going. I can remember nights that I sat up crying. I didn't know how I was going to make it through."

"I completely understand, Keisha. It has to be tough caring for a child and trying to earn a degree."

"You've got that right, Sean, especially when you don't have any help."

"Don't tell me that the father is a dead beat."

"Sean, that loser hasn't been involved since he found out that I was pregnant. He got into some trouble a few years ago, and the judge threw the book at his ass. He gave him five-to-ten. I have been raising Travis all by myself since. It was hard at first, but it gets easier every day.

"Damn, Keisha. I really commend you. God knows that I wouldn't know where to begin. I can't raise a dog let alone a child. You're my hero."

"Thanks, Sean. I am just a mother in love with her child. My little boy is so sweet to me. He's funny too. He's my little angel."

"You don't have to convince me, I believe you. If he is anything like you, then he has a sweet heart. Keep working with him."

"Well, I won't take up any more of your time. I know you have lots of people to see, Mr. Big Shot. So let's not make this awkward. Let's simply wish each other well and give each other a hug."

"Well said, Ms. Brown. You're the one that needs to be the author."

Keisha and I gave each other a warm hug and went our separate ways. Keisha failed at love but she was a fighter. The hurricane came and went. The clouds cleared, and when the rain settled, she was still standing. Keisha had been bruised, but she was still in place. Could I have done the same?

My stomach rumbled. Hunger pangs ate up my insides. I had to act fast or else the paroxysms and body convulsions would get worse. I could smell hickory and mesquite in the air. I spotted a heavyset man cooking a delicious bouquet of smoked meat. He roasted up pure goodness on a mammoth-sized grill.

In suburban areas, people went to the local hardware store to get cooking grills. They found traditional upright gas grills, whipped out their credit cards, and called it a day. In the city, the perfect grill looked completely different. They were created using hollowed truck mufflers. All grilling aficionados knew that the best barbeque came off truck muffler grills. Old folks called it a smoker. I knew that only one person was actually qualified to cook on it, Chris Banks.

Chris Banks was always the chubby kid. As a freshman, he easily weighed three hundred pounds. Like most of us, Chris had a nickname. We called him Jelly Roll. It may have seemed mean, but the nickname actually fit him well. Despite his size, all the girls thought he was quite the catch. He was handsome, and he could burn better than a woman as far as cooking was concerned.

Chris had fine wavy hair and gray eyes that chicks loved. He had a true appreciation for food. He started cooking at the age of eight and continued throughout high school. He went on to culinary arts school and graduated with high respect from his peers and instructors. Despite his weight, he was a Mack with the women. In the present, he still was heavy, but he looked well. Sitting behind him was a beautiful ass sister. She had a little bit of baby fat herself, but could model in any magazine she wanted. She was that attractive. She had long flowing hair with a soft curl in it and a gargantuan-sized wedding ring on her finger. She must have been Chris' wife. I watched him spoon-feed her barbeque sauce and confirmed it in my mind.

I headed over to talk to him. Chris was official; he was one of the first people that actually bought a copy of my first book. I wanted to let him know how much I appreciated it and congratulate him on becoming the new chef at the prestigious Franklin Eatery on Chicago's Gold Coast. Franklin's was arguably the best restaurant in the Midwest. All of the news stations voted it in the top five year after year. When Jelly Roll got the gig, all of the Chicago papers covered the story. Finally, one of Chicago's own earned the job. Upscale eateries like Franklin's usually chose chefs with European flair. They were from either Paris or Switzerland most of the time. Chris was now one of the country's elite. It was a real honor.

I went over and sparked up a conversation with him. I made a megaphone with my hands and started yelling.

"Introducing, Chicago's culinary extraordinaire and the new chef of Franklin's Eatery, ol' gray eyes himself, Mr. Jelly Roll!"

"Is that you, Sean? The earth must be standing still. I cannot believe it, Mr. Jiles."

Chris looked over towards me and burst out in laughter.

"You're damn right! It's me, in the flesh! What's good with you, my big homie?"

"I'm blessed, Sean; how about you?"

Chris was right. He was living his dream. He found something he loved and stuck with it. So many people are fearful; they don't have what it takes to become an expert at one thing. It took too much sacrifice. Chris did it though. He was a certified chef, and judging by the aroma's I smelled, was a damn good one!

"Sean, the last time I saw you in person was at the prom. I will never forget that jade green cummerbund and white patent leather slip on's you had on. If I had a dollar every time I laughed about how you looked in it, I would be a millionaire."

"Jelly Roll, laugh if you want to, but you know as well as I do that clothes like that were the shit back in the day! I was on my job that night. Don't hate."

"I'm not hatin'."

"Yes you are. Don't make me get on you. Look at what you had on; do I really have to go there. Jelly Roll?"

Chris looked back at the woman sitting behind him and started to blush. He reached forward, grabbed her hand and assisted her with standing up, then he spoke again.

"Sean, there's someone I want you to meet. This is my wife Layla. We have been married for three years now, and she is every bit of my better half."

Confirmed, he really was married. I was impressed! Jelly Roll had picked a winner. They looked perfect together.

"It's nice to meet you in person, Sean. Chris has told me so much about you.

She stood up and extended her hand to shake mine. I introduced myself and congratulated them on their union. Layla placed her hand on Jelly Roll's belly and began to rub circles on top of it as she simultaneously kissed him on the lips.

They looked like they were still in love with one another. I paid Chris' wife a few compliments and commented on her engagement ring. It was amazing. The ring was a Tiffany diamond in full brilliance. The blinding white light from the gemstone was enough to illuminate even the darkest room. The solitaire looked like a piece of heaven trapped on her finger.

"Sweet Jesus! Look at that ring; it looks like an iceberg ran into your finger. It's marvelous, Mrs. Banks."

"Why thank you, Sean. I have heard so much about you. Some of the stories Chris tells me about your high school days are unbelievable. You people had such a great time, Sean!

"Yes, we did!"

"Chris has a copy of your book in our library back home."

"Library, huh? Most people bought my book then left it in their cars or at work," I joked trying to downplay my literary success . Chris reengaged himself back into the conversation.

"You want something to eat?"

"I thought you'd never ask."

I piled rib tips, hot links, and burgers onto my plate, then devoured the barbeque just as fast as I piled it up on my plate.

"Your material is really good, Sean. My wife and I were in New York when the first set of reviews came out. All of the reviewers gave you five stars when they reviewed it. They even said you were going to be the next urban fiction icon. You should be proud of it."

I was flattered. I do remember how excited I was when I got the first set of reviews. I bought ten copies of the paper at the newsstand. I continued the conversation.

"Jelly Roll, man, these rib tips are off tha meter! You are the best cook I know, man. I am gonna have to check you out at Franklin's since you are the head honcho there. Now I have an excuse to fly back to Chicago. Mrs. Banks, I see why you married ol' gray eyes. After eating this, I want to marry him. Wow!"

We all burst out in laughter. I sopped up the last few morsels of barbeque goodness and wished them well. I gave them both a hug and moved towards the next group of people.

I wiped my hands with a moist paper towel. The sun was blazing. It got hotter by the second. The softball game would be starting soon. I removed my shirt and walked over to the baseball diamond wearing my tank top.

I spotted Josh near the dugout area. He had a huge bag filled with baseball equipment and accessories. He had caps, gloves, bats, balls, and even bases. Who walked around with actual bases in their bag?

"Josh! What's up, my brother?"

"Man, you know me, just trying to stay cool out here; it's hotter than a hundred jalapeños out here!"

"You've got that right; you see I had to come out of that shirt. I was about to have a heat stroke!"

"Are you ready for the game?"

"Sure am, you know I am tha bomb at sports."

"Well, Sean, I hope you brought you're a-game."

"Is it still guys against girls?"

"Yup, sure is."

"Sweet, then the girls are about to get their asses kicked!'

"Well, I don't know, Sean. Remember we modified the rules to make it fairer. To close an inning, the women only have to tag us out twice instead of three times. Then when they are on offense, they get one extra out, so we have to tag them out four times to close an inning."

"Damn! We are still in good shape though. It's doable."

"How's your mom?"

"She is good; I am going to stop by the house to see her later on."

"Sean, please tell me you didn't bring that crazy ass girlfriend of yours to our reunion."

"Nope."

"Good, I'm not in the mood to deal with attitude today, Sean. I am trying to have a good time. So should you."

"Oh yeah, Josh, I forgot to tell you. Eva and I broke up, man. I finally called it quits."

"Oh shit! Really?"

"Yup."

"Who dumped who?"

"If you must know, technically I dumped her."

Josh was stunned but thrilled. He has hated Eva since day one. He said that she was not worthy of his best friend. I quickly changed the subject.

"Who else have you seen so far at the reunion?"

"Come on, Sean, grow a set of balls and ask me what you really want to ask me."

Josh knew my question behind the question. I wanted to know if he had seen Jade. I wanted to know if he had seen her.

"I won't make you ask, Sean. The answer is yes. She is right over there by the opponents' dugout. She's their secret weapon."

"Jade is here?"

"I told you that you didn't have to ask. Yes, *your* Jade is here!"

I was speechless. Could Josh see it written all over my face? I looked across the field to confirm her presence and sure enough, it was Jade. She looked awesome. She looked even more beautiful than I remembered. She had the total package. I was in a daze. Josh spoke to me again.

"So are you ready to win this game. I want to mop the floor with the women!

"Be careful Josh, we've got liquor riding on this. Don't forget that the losing team has to buy the winning team a round of drinks at the bar, and if anyone could lead the women to victory, it was Jade. I began to get worried. For months, the men of Kensor's graduating class talked shit about how we were going to beat the women. We had to win.

Josh looked up at me with his signature smirk.

"We are gonna beat them like they stole something!"

Damn, Josh! He knew that Jade was going to be at the reunion and never told me. He knew that I still had feelings for her. I did not want our first meeting after more than five years of separation to consist of us staring at one another from across the dugout trying to read one another for a competitive advantage. On the other hand, I was overjoyed. As much as I wanted to win the softball game, I already felt triumphant, because I had another chance to see Jade. It didn't matter who won the game, because even if I lost, I was victorious.

Chapter 16
Dinner with Mama

"Mama, I'm home!"

"Oh my Lord, it's so good to see you, Sean."

"Mama, I've missed you. How have you been?"

"I'm blessed and highly favored. And how are you doing these days?"

"I am beat, Mama. Do you remember the picnic I told you about?"

"Yes."

"Well, it turned out to be great. We even played a game of softball. Maybe I overdid it, because my body is aching."

"Sean, you ought to be ashamed of yourself. One of these days you are going to hurt yourself; you're not a teenager anymore. I have some Epsom salt in the linen closet if you want to run yourself a quick bath."

" Nah, Mama, I'm okay."

"So who won the game, Sean?"

"What did you say? Huh?"

"You heard me the first time. Don't play crazy with me, boy. Who won the game, the women or the men?"

"Well, what had happened was," I joked.

"The women must have won."

"Yes, ma' am, they did. They played awesome."

"They must have had some good players."

I scratched my forehead.

"Yeah, they did."

I didn't tell Mama that Jade played and hit two home runs and even a grand slam. "What are you cooking? The kitchen smells good!"

I looked over to the center island and saw two huge brown paper bags filled to the brim with groceries. There were enough provisions in the bags to feed a football team. Mama set the dining table. She had votive candles and even a centerpiece. It looked amazing. Mama had sweet potatoes, country ham, a few ears of corn, and a twenty-dollar pot roast in her sacks. So many food items spilled out of the bags and onto the countertop.

"It is a special occasion. My only son is home for the weekend. It is only fitting to make sure he gets a good home cooked meal. Besides, you know I love to cook. In fact, the more I come to think about it, other than a few church members, I really don't have much company at the house. I don't do much else. I'll sit on my porch, watch my stories, and look after that crazy dog, but that's about it"

"Tell me anything, Mama; I'm sure you have company over here all the time. I remember those nights you and Daddy fried fish and had people over for cards. The neighbors used to smell those aromas and come running. They almost broke their necks trying to get over here."

I tried to make Mama feel special. She truly was the best cook and host on the planet. My father once told me that Mama's beauty caught his eye, but it was her cooking that made him fall in love with her. My daddy grew up very poor. He lived in the housing projects for the better part of his youth. His family never had much to work with. All they had was their love. He learned at an early age that the simple pleasures in life were most valuable. My father was a giving man. When he met Mama, he showered her with gifts every chance he had. He bought her jewelry, flowers, and candy. He was a world class romantic that was butter smooth. He loved Mama so deeply. He would do anything for her or destroy anyone that tried to harm her.

Mama and Daddy had a whirlwind romance. They experienced many firsts together. If he were still alive, he would be embarrassed to tell anyone, but until he turned twenty-two, he had never eaten in a real restaurant before. He was never able to afford it, but when he and my mother were courting, she took him to one for the first time.

Back in the day, Mama worked on the wait staff at a restaurant downtown. The restaurant was near Grant Park, and it was very classy. One evening Mama stayed late and snuck Daddy in after the restaurant closed. She prepared him a gourmet meal and served it to him. They sat at the best table in the house. They feasted on a five-course meal complete with a julienne salad, cream of cheddar broccoli soup, chicken vescuvio, a mini-Black Forest cake with cherry glaze, and coffee. My father told me that he knew right then that Mama would be his wife. My mother spoke and snapped me back to the present.

"Whatever, Sean, nobody comes over here. Lord knows I haven't had a dinner date since, well you know. I'm just making sure my baby gets what he needs. You can't trust these processed foods; there's no telling what folks put in them. Besides, nowadays folks have to make appointments to catch up with you. Ever since the good Lord blessed you with a way to make that stage play, you have been busy."

"Mama, you can say that again. Some nights I get so into my writing that look up and its morning. By the way, I have almost completed my manuscript. I just have to figure out how to end the story."

"Baby, that's so exciting, I am so proud of you. Every day I pray for you and ask God to bless all that you do. He has really blessed us."

"Amen! You're right, every day I thank God. Because of sacrifices you and Daddy made over the years, I am able to live out my dreams. You two gave me a chance that not many receive. I am so grateful for that. One day I am going to buy you that diner off Highway 57 that you've always wanted. Just wait and see!"

"Baby, I'm happy with things just as they are. I couldn't be more pleased. You're the first college graduate in the family, you believe in God, and as far as I know, you are staying out of trouble. Aren't you?"

"Mama, you know I stay away from trouble."

"You sure?'

"Yes, Ma'am, I wouldn't lie to you. That one incident in high school was enough to scare me straight."

"I'll bet it was. I could have strangled you that night, Sean."

My mother started laughing and nearly lost her footing."

"Be careful, Mama, you almost fell down."

I have always been on the straight and narrow. I have always kept my head low and stayed under the radar when it came to nonsense. To avoid the temptation I kept my mind occupied at all times. Between drama club, my writing, and school classes, I stayed as busy as a cat covering up shit. There was only one exception, the Winter Ball Dance during my junior year.

The Winter Ball was a coming of age event for the junior class. We all wanted to be grown and sexy. The young women wore provocative dresses that were excessively skimpy. They showed entirely too much cleavage. All of the young men dressed fresh. Since we had driver's licenses, we all came to the dance driving either a rental or a borrowed set of wheels. My mother had a brand new limited edition luxury sedan that was fully loaded. It had a sunroof, leather seats, a premium sound system, and a keyless entry system. My mother even got the optional voice kit that said the direction the car was traveling in, if a door was ajar, and when the fuel tank was low on gas. It was the perfect vehicle for the dance, but my mother wasn't letting me near it.

The Junior Prom was an important time for me. Two weeks before the dance I built up the nerve to ask the captain of the pompom team to be my date. She was one of the hottest girls in school, and to my surprise, she said yes. She was a stallion. If my mother had seen her, she would have called her loose. She oozed sex appeal. I figured that if I showed up at her door driving a luxury whip and looking handsome, she would let me hit. I was so naïve.

Since my mother wouldn't give me the keys and let me borrow the car, I came up with an elaborate scheme to sneak it out of the garage, have my fun, and get it back home before she even noticed. I rehearsed the heist a full week in advance to make sure I had it down to the tee.

The Reunion

The dance fell on a Friday night, the same evening as the weekly *Women's Only* church service. The church was only three blocks away from the house, so my mother never drove. Even on the coldest days, she walked. She said it kept her young and gave her a chance to get in touch with Christ before the service.

The services had been a huge success since their inception. Every week the pews were packed with supporters. The pastor, Elder Light, was a firm believer in giving both men and women a separate opportunity to cleanse their spirits without the occasional distraction that the opposite sex can pose to the will of God. He came up with the idea to do separate services after a Jezebel-like vixen walked into the service wearing a skintight outfit that had nearly half the congregation's men drooling in lust. She was red hot! She must have been in search of a husband. Either that or she was a professional streetwalker, because the outfit she had on was very inappropriate for church. Back in the day, we used to call them cat suits. They were made of either soft leather or latex and hugged a woman's body. They left nothing to the imagination.

She was ripe fruit. She was perfect for the hood star awards. The entire congregation noticed. Women hissed like snakes, and the men all spoke with their eyes. That day nobody paid attention to the Word of God. No one left with the message that the pastor blessed them with. Instead, they all left talking about the vixen. Pastor was embarrassed and offended. He started the separate services the following week.

Technically, church service lasted two hours, but when you added in church announcements, the building fund progress report, and selections by the women's faith choir, service was extended to three or four hours easy. That was enough time to pick up my date, have a good time, and bring my mama's whip back without her noticing it was gone. With Mama at church I could floss and live the life of a grown up. The car fit me perfectly. It was midnight black and damned near matched my skin tone. It had chrome accents and was very elegant. People would mistake me for a corporate executive.

Everything was clockwork. On the day of the dance, my mother left for church. My mother knew nothing about the dance, or so I thought. I never mentioned it to her. For all she knew I was at home playing video games. I was so sneaky back then.

As soon as she walked out of the door, I worked my plan. I had my wallet, house keys, dance tickets, and date's address all in hand. I got dressed and walked out of the door. I took a mental picture of my surroundings. My mom was keen at noticing things that were out of place. She was a super sleuth. I grabbed my mom's spare car key. She showed me where she hid it in case there was ever an emergency.

I went into the garage. I marveled at the breathtaking vehicle. It looked like wet licorice. I matched the car with my signature black suit. I had on a white collared shirt and a black tie. I looked like a CIA agent.

I opened the garage door and hopped in the driver's seat. I turned on the radio and cranked up the music as loud as it could go. I exited the garage and found my favorite station. Young folks loved 88.1FM, because they played all of the latest hits. Their deejays were loud and ghetto, but they were the number one rated radio station in all of Chicago.

I closed the garage door. I sped off in a fury and drove down my block like a lunatic. I did fifty miles per hour in a thirty mile per hour zone. I made it to the expressway; I did eighty miles an hour when sixty-five would have sufficed. I made it to my date's house in eleven minutes. My date lived in a bad neighborhood, so instead of getting out the car and walking up to her porch and ringing the bell, I simply honked my horn and waited for her to come out. Thank heaven she was ready. I saw her waiting by the bay window. She had on a banging outfit. She looked so sexy. She hurried out to the car. I unlocked the doors, and she got in. I sped off in arrogant fashion. I thought I was on top of the world. All the goons on her block estimated me as I drove down the street in my vessel.

"Hey, Sean! You look so nice, baby. This car is the shit!"

"Thank you, thank you. You know I had to clean up nice for you, baby cakes."

My date was a little materialistic, but she was cool. At seventeen, who didn't care about labels, brand names, and appearances? She was one-dimensional, nonetheless, certainly girlfriend material. I stroked her ego and played the part. I drove down the highway and tried to look as cool as I could. My ladybird sat shotgun. We looked great together. Our outfits matched and everything.

"Sean, I can't wait 'til my friends see us get out of this car. They are going to freak out."

"I bet they will."

I was no fool, she used me because I had a set of wheels, but I used her too. When my friends saw me with her, they were going to freak. I would get a million cool points. My date was an upgrade from the type of girls I usually I hung out with. I dated artsy chicks. Girls who played violin, oil painted, wrote poetry, and sang. Those girls were cute at best, far from red-hot. Mentally they were the upper crust, but physically they were far from sexy. Artsy chicks found their sexiness later on in life.

We made it to the party in no time. I pulled to the front entrance and made a grand entrance. Across the street from the dining hall was a French bistro with valet service. For ten dollars, they would park one's car in high style. I opted for the flashy service. The main parking booth was in plain sight of the student entrance for the party. If I parked there, everyone would see us.

"Let's use the valet service. I don't feel like finding a space tonight."

"Okay, big baller, shot caller. Sean, you are turning me on with all of this flashiness. I never knew you had this much class."

Ooh yeah, girl, run that game. My plan was working!

In no time, she was putty in my hands.

"That'll be ten dollars, sir. Please take this ticket, and when you return, please give it to the valet attendant. They will get your car and pull it around for you."

The valet attendant looked me in the eyes and smirked. He was a young man too. He knew the car wasn't mine

"Thank you, sir.." I said announcing my gratitude instead of being modest.

"Thank you, sir."

I gave him a five and winked my right eye at him like he and I had a connection. Then I walked away.

"You ready, baby?"

"Oh hell yeah. Do you think anybody saw us get out of the car? My nosey ass girlfriends see everything. They don't miss a beat."

"Maybe they did, maybe they didn't; who cares? Let's just go in and have a good time."

My phony comment came across viscerally and as unbroken as Egyptian silk. My date acknowledged my statement.

"You're right, Sean. Let's just go in. I feel kinda silly standing out here in the cold, waiting to see if someone saw us. Can you dance, Sean?"

"Nah, but I can two-step."

My date laughed. The two-step was a lifesaver. It was the only dance that allowed a person who couldn't dance worth shit to fake it and still look cool.

We walked into the banquet hall, wide-eyed. The decorations were exquisite. The early Roman inspired architecture looked classy.

I saw my best friend Josh in the crowd. He and his girlfriend, Constance, walked over to us. Josh smirked at me from afar.

"What's good, Josh?"

"Nothing much. What's up with you, Sean?"

"Nothing much, I'm just chillin'. Constance, you look nice."

"Thanks, Sean. You are dapper yourself. You look clean in that suit."

Josh looked my date up and down. He stared at her bosom and at her bottom. Constance noticed Josh drooling, so she immediately went into bitch mode. Constance was on the committee, so she could use that as an excuse to get her man away from the threat that was my date.

"Josh, come with me to the registration table. I need to check on some things."

"One second, honey. I would like to meet Sean's guest."

"Josh, it's cool, I will catch up with you guys later."

"No, Sean, please introduce me to your friend. I don't know if I've ever had the pleasure?"

"Well, if you insist. Josh this is--"

Constance interrupted.

"Josh, we need to get over to the greeters' table. I have to hand out name tags. Plus I'm thirsty and could really use some punch. Can you get me some?"

Constance was no fool. Anybody with eyes that worked saw how gorgeous my date was. Josh may have been in a relationship, but he wasn't blind. Constance had plenty of sense too. She knew that she had to distract Josh and pull his attention away from my date's physique. Josh exploded.

"Damn, Constance, we just came from over there. Why do we need to go back?"

My buddy asked the question aloud, but he knew why she wanted them to go to the opposite end of the room. The tension was getting thick, so I intervened.

"Josh, it's cool. I will find time later, seriously. We have take pictures anyway. Let's catch up later on."

"Aiight, Sean."

"Okay, Josh. Bye, Constance."

We danced the night away and had a good time. When it was time to go, I summoned my date. She was with her pompom buddies, chatting it up. I walked over to her.

"Baby, it's time to go."

"Sean, can I get the car from the valet?"

"Are you crazy? I'm not letting you drive that car. Why would you even fix your lips to ask me such a silly question?"

My date started pouting. She puckered her lips and begged me again in front of her friends.

"Come on, Sean; let me bring the car around. I've never driven a car that nice, and I just want to wrap my hands around that thick black steering wheel. We can go to the lakefront and chill. Maybe even do some other things if you're lucky."

She knew that she could switch me on with her body movements. I went senseless. I started thinking with the wrong head.

I looked her square in the eye and tried to think of an excuse, but I could not come up with one. This was not some hooptie on the street. It was my mother's car. If she wrecked it, I would get my ass kicked for sure. I mustered up the best excuse I could think of.

"Baby, I don't care about you bringing up the car. It's just that I don't want you to catch a cold out there. It's cold. I'll go get it."

My date reached for her coat and snatched my keys. She darted out of the building and yelled back at me.

"I'll get the car! I can't help it! I'll be right back!"

"Hey!"

I was shocked. She jacked me for my keys. As I watched her run in heels, I had to admit that she looked sexy as hell running in that skin tight dress.

Her ass swayed from side to side as she scampered through the hallway and ran out the door. When we first arrived, the skies were clean and clear. By the time the dance was over, it was a full-fledged blizzard. There had to be at least six-inches of snow on the ground. I grew nervous. My date was young and naïve, one false move, and she could wreck my mama's wheels.

I ran to the front entrance and waited for her to pull up the car. I hoped to God that the car was still in one piece. Five minutes passed, and there was no sign of the car. I grew skittish with each passing minute. *Where was she?* I was at the end of my wits when she finally pulled up. I ran over to the driver's side door and opened it. I tried not to make a scene, but anxiety was written all over my face. I flung the door open and grabbed my date's arm.

"Where the hell did you go?" I was upset and relieved.

"Sean, relax, I didn't crash your car. Everything is fine."

"You're the one that needs to relax."

I was about to piss on myself. I checked the car for dents and dings. I saw none.

"Sean, I showed the car off to a few of my friends. The car is beautiful. I couldn't resist."

What an irony. I had no right to be upset with her, because I did the same thing. The car wasn't mine, it belonged to my mother."

"Sweetie, you are a mess. You are lucky you came back. You were about to get it."

My date saw me soften up. I went from mad to lovey-dovey in one minute. My lady-friend's blatant risk taking turned me on. My date apologized. She told me that she would make it up to me.

"Sean, why don't we go to the lakefront so we can chill?"

"There's like six-inches of snow outside."

"Exactly. We will have the entire lakefront all to ourselves."

"Sure!"

I charged up. I could feel my nature rising. She was talking my language. She knew I wanted her. I hit the expressway and drove to Lake Shore Drive. It was so cold outside. The blizzard hit the city hard. Snowflakes were so large that they began to camouflage my windshield.

I made it to the beach in no time. I pulled into the parking lot and found a perfect parking space. It was towards the end of the lot near a secluded area. No one could see us; we could get away with anything. I put the car in park, turned the lights off, and kept the engine keep running with the heat on. The games began.

"So, Sean, you really liked my outfit, huh?"

"Of course, you looked great tonight."

"I only look great tonight?"

"You look great every day; I noticed it even more this evening."

"Well, why don't you take a closer look at me?"

Sensations rushed through my body. Her beauty was unmatched. Her chocolate brown skin was beautiful and nearly as dark as mines. Her sexy almond shaped bedroom eyes seduced me. Her smile was flirtatious, and she even had the nerve to have dimples. Her hair was whipped and styled just the way I liked. For that moment, she was perfect to me. I adored her carefree attitude, and if I had my wish, I would make her mine.

I wasted no time. I removed the top of her dress and unclipped her bra. Her breasts were exposed and ready to be suckled. I could not believe how faultless her nipples were. They were large and erect. My adolescent eyes gazed at them mystified. Truth be told I had only seen a set of real titties in person twice and one of those times was when I was a baby.

I conjured up the nerve to go further. She let me. I could not believe she was as into me as she was.

151

"Damn, girl, you look amazing. Your body is so perfect," I said in a raspy tone. I read somewhere that women preferred men with deep voices over men with high-pitched ones. I tried my damndest to reach the low register but could only muster a baritone.

"So do you like what you see, Sean?"

"Yes, I do, baby."

My date turned me on with her seductive line of questioning. I was as hard as a rock. I knew she saw my dick imprint on my slacks. The lump swelled in my pants.

"Sean, you smell so good to me."

I kissed her on the nape of her neck and touched her skin softly. My date placed her hands on my penis and stroked me through my pants.

"Based on what I feel, you *definitely* like what you see."

I remained calm on the outside, but on the inside, I was terrified. I was a virgin And my dick was harder than four Ferrari payments. I had seen sex performed before on smut movies so how hard could it be? Although I was a rookie, having sex seemed like an easy enough thing to do. It wasn't like I never tried to have sex, it just never occurred. I never made it past first base. The closest I came was with my sophomore year girlfriend. It was a complete disaster and a waste of a perfectly good rubber. I knew nothing about the joys of having sex. I snapped out of my daydream.

"Hmm, yeah, it certainly feels like you are working with a little sumthin, sumthin."

"Want me to show it to you?"

"Sean, wait. There is something I have to tell you."

My sweetheart took her hands off my manhood and leaned back onto her seat. I began to get nervous.

"Sean, I'm a virgin."

"What?"

"Yeah, I have never had sex before."

"But you were just…"

"I know, I know. Believe me, I'm cool with kissing a little bit, and maybe a little touching, but I'm not ready to have sex, especially not tonight...in a car!"

I was shocked but relieved. None of my boys knew I was still a virgin. Every time the topic of sex came up in the locker room or in the hallways before class, I always lied. They all thought I had been with dozens of girls when I hadn't even been with one.

"Sean, maybe this was a bad idea. I'm just not ready. You're not mad are you?"

Whew!

"Girl, you have no idea."

I stuffed my sausage back into my pants and confessed the truth to her.

"Don't worry about it. Since we are being honest, let me let you in on a little secret. I'm a virgin too."

"What? I don't believe it. All the girls at school said that you were a real pro and that you had been with at least a dozen girls."

"Really? Well that shit is a lie."

"I have never even seen a real coochie up close. I was just as nervous as you were. Look at me, I am still shaking."

"This is trippy. Are you for real? You are really a virgin too?"

"Yes."

All of a sudden, my date grabbed me by the collar and started to French kiss me again, only this time it was much harder. I gladly returned affection to her. We kissed for almost five minutes straight.

"What was that for?"

"I am just so happy right now. You are a special boy."

"I am not that special, you better not tell anybody. I would be so mortified if people knew the truth."

"Your secret is safe with me."

We both started cracking up. We laughed like we were watching a comedy special. Her honesty was refreshing. I had pegged her all wrong. She was someone I could see myself dating. I went out on a limb.

"Would you be my girlfriend?"

"You mean as in like boyfriend and girlfriend?"

"Yeah silly."

"You want to be my boyfriend?"

"Yes I do."

My sweetie pie blushed and leaned over to kiss me on the cheek then responded, "Yes, I'll be your girlfriend."

I felt like the happiest man on earth. One would think that I had proposed to her and she said yes. My date looked down at the clock and her eyes nearly popped out of their sockets.

"Oh shit! I have to get home. I am about to miss my curfew!"

Her outburst startled me. I regained my composure and remembered my own deception. I needed to get Mama's car back home before church let out. The clock read 10:35 p.m.

"What time is your curfew, sweetie pie?"

"My curfew is eleven o'clock, no ifs, ands, or buts. My daddy will kick my ass if I'm not back at the house in time. In fact, he may even kick yours too."

"We can't have that. Your ass is too nice to be kicked. It needs to be felt on, not kicked."

She smiled, kissed me on the cheek then urged me to jet.

"Baby, stop kidding around, we need to go."

"You're right, you're right. I have to get back home too. Tthis car needs to be in the garage in about an hour."

"What time is your curfew, Sean?"

"I don't have a curfew," I lied, trying to sound grown.

I cut the car back on and backed out of the parking space. I exited the lot and headed southbound. My date's house was only ten minutes away from where we were. She stayed on the East side of Chicago near Jeffrey Boulevard. I did fifty miles an hour on the highway while watching my sweetheart put her half-removed clothing back on. She reaffixed her brassier and situated her dress. Every few seconds I snuck peeks.

I made it to her spot quickly despite the snow.. I stopped in front of her house and glanced down at the clock again. It read 10:50 p.m. We made it! I did not want our night to end, but it did. My date hopped out of my car, gave me an air kiss and a smile then ran into the house to make curfew.

"See you on Monday, boyfriend!"

"Bye, Jade."

I was scared as heck. I had to make it all the way back to the far Southside in ten minutes. I drove like a bat out of hell. I ran stop signs, sped through yellow lights, and zoomed past pedestrians. I was glad that I didn't kill someone that night. Thank God, Mama was at church praying for me. I made it all the way back to my house with no issues. The car was in tact, the gas gauge had barely moved, and the car was unscathed. The car had no dents, dings or scratches. That was until I tried to park the car in the garage.

I opened the garage door and put the car in reverse to pull inside. I inched in ever so carefully and made sure I didn't brush the car against the sides of the garage. What I didn't notice was a large patch of black ice hidden on the ground just underneath the tires of the car. I don't know how it happened, or why it happened to me for that matter, all I know is that when I hit the gas the car slid about ten feet from where I was. The entire left side of Mama's car was scratched up all to be damned. I pissed my pants, literally.

My mother's car was fucked up! The paint job was ruined. It looked like someone took a giant fingernail file to it. Her luxury sedan looked like a bumper car. I was scared shitless. However, even in my most panicked states, I always found ways to pull it together and remain calm.

I had a backup plan. I parked the car anyhow, snuck my pissy ass back into the house, and decided to play crazy. If Mama asked me about the damage to the car, I would act like I was clueless to the fact. It wasn't like my mother knew that I took the car. We did live in a questionable neighborhood. I could blame it on that. It wasn't far fetched to say a vagrant snuck into the garage and fucked the car up, looking for money to score their next hit.

I closed the garage door, hurried across the back lawn, and snuck into my bedroom window. My heart raced. I looked down to my watch I noticed that it read 10:59 p.m.

Mama would be home soon, or so I thought. Little did I know that Mama was waiting for me in the darkness. She switched my bedroom light on and started yelling. My mother stood in the doorway holding a leather belt. She still had her purple church hat on.

"Sean! Where have you been?"

"Mama, I...I...I..."

I was speechless.

"Why are you climbing through a window?"

I continued stuttering.

"Ooh Jesus, I am gonna kick the living shit out of you if you don't answer me!"

"Mama, you just got out of church..."

Even in my darkest hour, I was a true smart ass. I could make stupid remarks in my sleep. I tried to muster up a statement, but I could not. Then at the most inopportune time, my mother's spare car key fell out of my pocket and onto the bedroom floor. It was in plain sight. Mama was no fool. Once she saw the key, she knew what I had done..

"Is that my car key? Were you driving my car?"

"Yes."

"Did something happen to my car? Is that why your stupid ass tried to sneak back into the house through the window?"

I was scared stiff. I reached down to pick up the car key, but my mother snatched it before I could pick it up. She ran out of the house into the snow wearing that purple church hat. I was petrified. My mother ran across the lawn and opened the garage.

"Oh Lord! Help me! Jesus, I'm gonna kill him!"

I got my ass whooped seven times that night. She even woke me up out of my sleep to run that belt across my ass. Fixing the damages cost me one thousand one hundred dollars. I used half a summer's savings to pay back my mother.

She never knew that I took the car to be with Jade. She never asked me the reason why I took it, but I think she always knew. My mother was wise and knew me better than I knew myself.

I snapped back into reality. It was time to eat. I gazed out the window. I saw that she had the same car from back in the day. It looked just as flawless as it did back then. I continued my discussion with Mama.

"Mama, I'm so sorry about what I did to your car that time. I was young and dumb. I should have never taken your car. It was disrespectful and dishonest."

"Baby, I told you a long time ago, don't worry about it. I forgive you. It's just a car. I'm just glad you didn't get hurt that night."

'I did get hurt."

"I am not talking about the whoopin' I put on your bottom. I'm talking about getting hurt on the road, silly. Besides, I know why you did it. It was for that girl."

"Geez, Mama. How did you know? You must have a gift."

"Baby, I have always known. Jade is a sweet girl now, and she was a sweet girl then. Too bad you two never made anything of your relationship. You and Jade seemed good for one another. Too bad y'all broke it off. That's a shame, after everything you two have been through. Wasn't she your prom date too?"

"Yeah, but that was a long time ago. Things are complicated. We tried dating in college, and it just...well... it's hard to explain.

I will always love her, but--"

"Sweety, you don't owe me any explanation. Everything happens for a reason, remember that."

"I know, Mama."

My mother hit a nerve talking about Jade. Out of all the relationships I had been involved in, the one with Jade was the one that I missed the most. I should have said what was on my heart, but when the time came, I didn't. Everything must happen for a reason.

"Baby, you should go get cleaned up, dinner will be ready in a few minutes."

"Okay, Mama."

I took a quick shower then came back to the dining room. I felt like Daddy at that table. For three hours my mother and I feasted on excellence. Mama and I caught up on the last few years of my life. I imagined Daddy smiling at us from across the table. She looked as elegant and as strong as I remembered. I admired her for that. Jade embodied those qualities. She was so much like Mama.

We sat at the dining room eating, laughing, and telling stories for hours. We even put on a few records and danced the night away to old jazz. Things in my life were definitely confusing, but at least for those moments, everything in life was simple again.

Chapter 17
The Bachelor Party

I made it to Josh's bachelor party in no time. Mama had stuffed me so good that I could barely walk. Her home cooking was no joke. I walked into Hotel Karma feeling like a Thanksgiving bird. The hotel was sexy. It seemed like I was in some foreign land. The décor looked Egyptian. All of the sofas were savory red, the carpet was a deep purple, and the walls were covered in marigold paint. The hotel certainly lived up to its title.

In addition to their regular rooms, Hotel Karma had a dozen executive level suites, each with their own theme and special name. The best suite was The Love Temple. We chose that room for Josh's bachelor party. The room had sex appeal. Two oversized doors secured the grandiose entranceway of the penthouse suite. I walked towards the entrance and saw two men dressed in black. They frisked people at the door. The muscle-bound security guards looked like they were cage fighters. They looked like they were ready to take *any* muthafucka out that acted the fool.

"May we help you?"

"I'm Sean Jiles. I am the co-host of the party."

"One moment please. I need to check the list."

"No problem, fellas, I don't want no trouble with you Hercules looking fools."

"There you are. I've found your name. Mr. Jiles, welcome to the party. The guest of honor arrived a few minutes ago. Go on in, sir."

"Thank you. I see you two aren't fuckin' around this evening. Keep up the good work and remember, if anyone gets out of hand, kick ass first and ask questions later. You have my blessing."

"Yessir!"

"By the way, sir, this place is exquisite."

"Indeed it is. Anything for my best friend."

I tipped the security team and gave them a twenty-dollar bill each since it seemed like they were on their square and doing their duty. When I designed Josh's party, I made sure to have plenty of security. I wasn't planning on having any bullshit. I wanted to make sure that Josh had a fun and safe atmosphere for his guests. Josh appreciated it too. The last time we were at a bachelor party together, three people got injured, and more than a dozen were hauled off to jail for fighting over one of the strippers. The man couldn't keep his hands to himself. He overdid it, and the performers went back and told their pimp. The pimp came out to the foyer and saw the man wildin' out. The drunkard couldn't keep it in his pants. He tried to stick his erect penis into some girl's booty hole. What a creep!

Some guys just don't get it. Stripping is all about creating the fantasy. Perhaps there are a few out there willing to give happy endings, but for the most part, most of the professional strippers that performed at bachelor parties didn't get down and dirty. The filthy man didn't subscribe to that line of thinking. He exposed his erect penis and the pimp cold-cocked his ass. He had the shit knocked out of him!

Anytime people mixed half-naked women with drunken men, the recipe spelled disaster. I didn't want to have anything like that go down at Josh's shindig. I walked into the hotel room. It looked exactly like the brochure. Putting a bachelor party together using only the internet was hard work. I deserved a drink. I grabbed a bottle of distilled vodka and a glass filled with ice from the bar area and searched the hotel suite for Josh. I found him.

"Sean! Things are about to be off the meter!

I surveyed the room. It looked like Josh had invited half the earth. Back in high school, he was the guy that knew everybody. He was also the one who had all the girls. Seeing him in action was amazing. He wasn't a pretty boy, he didn't play sports, and he didn't come from money. Josh didn't even have a car, but he became the most popular guy at school. I had the yearbook to prove it.

Josh was a smooth bastard. He had a silver tongue. He could talk to anyone. He was cultivated. Josh could strike up conversation with anyone. He had something in common with everybody. He was one of the few people on the planet that was successful at anything they chose to do or be. He stood six foot two with a solid build. He wasn't an arrogant tough guy, but he could scrap with the best of them. He sang in the choir and performed in talent shows so that also helped his persona. I bet all the girls used to cream on themselves whenever he sang ballads in the hallways. All of those things got Josh noticed, but what made him popular was his parties.

Every week Josh threw a party. He alternated between his mother's garage and his grandfather's fishing cabin on the lake.

The Reunion

Josh's mother worked nights, and his grandfather preferred to stay in the city. Every Saturday evening, kids from all over the neighborhood showed their love by attending Josh's soirees. The finest girls in the city showed up for Josh's parties. I don't know what he used to say to those girls to get them to show up, but they did. Dozens came each week.

Josh's suave came naturally. Cool was like his second skin, and he really worked it. Nobody hated on Josh. His silkiness was evident. I wasn't blind; I knew cool when I saw it. Josh's day job was theater, but at night, he used his swagger to pioneer his own hip-hop themed handbag line. He met with the right people and said all the right things. He put out his line, and a few years later, a major name label purchased his line. They distributed the gear nationwide. A chain of well-known department stores even featured Josh's designs with displays. I was happy for him, genuinely happy. Josh had come a long way. He wasn't a millionaire, but he made enough to live well.

Josh had the power. All he needed was a woman to share his life. He found her! Josh proposed to his Constance, and she gleefully accepted. I promised Josh that if he ever got married, I would put together a bachelor party for him.

"So, Josh, are you ready for your big day?"

"I'm ready; Constance is the one."

"What are you sippin' on?"

"I've got myself some of that good brown liquor."

Out of nowhere, a man with finger waves in his hair yelled at the top of his lungs on what appeared to be a sequin covered microphone. The microphone was money green in color with the word PIMP inscribed on both sides.

"Are y'all drunk muthafuckas ready to get started?"

The crowd responded and he spoke again.

"Dammit, I said, are ya'll ready to get shit crackin'? If so, let me hear you say yeah!" The crowd yelled back again.

The hype man yelled out one last time to the crowd.

"Are ya'll ready to see some titties, ass, and sweet pussy?"

The crowd yelled back in unison, "Hell yeah!"

The room went pitch black. The DJ started mixing and scratching on his turntables. All of a sudden, the subwoofers started beating and pounding. Sensual music played in the background.

The DJ spoke to the crowd one final time before he ensued.

"Fellas, introducing the sexiest, freakiest, thickest, and nastiest strippers in Chicago. Give a round of applause for some real pussy power. Get your money ready. Let's make it rain! Someone has to help these hoes pay for coll ege!

The crowd grew roudy. Jodi Proper, a real life pimp, sat in the corner and kept an eye on his flock. He was mighty with his pimp game. Jodi Proper was as well-known in Chicago as deep-dish pizza. I never wanted to be a pimp myself, but one had to respect him. It took quite a mouthpiece to convince a woman to sell *her* body for sex and turnaround and give *you* the money. Jodi had to be at least fifty years old, but he had a mean swagger. He looked straight out of a Blaxploitation film. Even looking at him was hard. Jodi had on a sunshine yellow suede suit with oversized bell-bottom trousers and a zebra print vest. His chest hair stuck out and a gold nameplate medallion from a Cuban link chain. He had one of those goofy ass pimp cups, and he reeked of cheap cologne and cigar smoke. He epitomized pimpology.

The DJ cued up each performer's music. One by one, vixens came out wearing their very best lingerie. I was ready. We all were.

The music continued to play while one participant holding bottles of Hennessey in each hand went around the room and poured shots of booze for everyone interested. The DJ played House music. It provoked the inner freak in everyone. Only in Chicago could a song called *I'll Beat that Bitch with a Bat, Let Them Hoes Fight,* or *It's Time for the Percolator* become a city-wide anthem.

The party was amazing. I was half-drunk and horny. I couldn't wait for the strippers to come out to put on a show for us. Josh gave me a high five.

"Now this is what I am talkin' about! Sean, you are tha man!"

"What'd I tell you? I told you that your bachelor party was gonna be off tha chain! Did you see the strippers come in?"

"Who didn't? I almost came on myself when they walked in. I can't wait to see them in their hoe outfits!"

"I'm just glad to be here celebrating with you, man!"

" I'm glad you could make it. It wouldn't be a party without you here, Sean. You might not be able to tell because I am drunk, but this really means the world to me!"

"Come on, Josh, don't hit me with that sentimental shit now. Get your dollars out. I am gonna tip some hoes tonight. Watch me go broke in this bitch! Watch me!"

"I bet you are, man. I am still kind of nervous about the wedding. I really want my marriage to work."

"Come on now. Stop that foolish talk, Josh. What you are doing is historic! You made the right choice. Constance is a great woman. You two complement each other so well."

"I know, Sean, I just don't want it to fail. Marriage is a sacred thing. I believe in it. My grandparents have been married for more than fifty years."

"I know what you mean, Josh. In my family, marriage is respected. Nobody here will tell you, but we all want what you have someday."

"See, Sean, that's why you need to keep writing and doing your stage plays. You say some really profound stuff sometimes. I feel better already."

"I am just being me."

"The music stopped. Click-clack noises from heels approached form the foyer. Strobe lights began to flash. A redbone chick wearing a red thong and a mask danced first. She had short platinum blonde hair. She had a navel ring and a voluptuous bottom. Four more women stood behind her, each with their own special outfit. There was a naughty nurse, a student, an attorney, and even a police office. Wow!

I continued my conversation with Josh.

"Let me ask you something, Josh."

"Speak ya mind."

"How did you know that Constance was the one?"

"It's kinda like there's this special switch inside your body that only she can click on. Everything becomes clear. Life gets easy. You just know."

"Really?"

"Yeah."

"Can you get any more specific? You sound like a politician."

"Well, I knew that my fiancée was the one right away. When I am around her, everything is calm. I can focus. Life feels like it is a joyride and not a bungee jump. She makes everything easier for me. There is no more drama in my life, no fighting, and no fussing. Most of all, I love her. I would do anything for her."

"Deep. That was profound, Josh."

For the next three hours, we drank, smoked cigars, and joked about old times. Most of the guests didn't leave until the break of dawn. I looked down at my watch. It read 4:00 a.m. I crashed in the spare bedroom in Josh's suite.. Josh knew that some of us would be too drunk to drive, so he took car keys from everyone. During the party, I drank two fifths of whiskey. I can remember stumbling around in the dark trying to find a pillow. I was so drunk that I even thought I saw Eva's crazy ass at the party walk in and go into a dark room with some guy. As tall as the man was, I thought he was Tommy Cole from our graduating class. Tommy Cole was hard to miss. He was almost seven feet tall. He played on the hoop squad at Kensor. He had a reputation for fucking anything that walked. *Good for him.* At least somebody got lucky. The woman he was with had big titties and looked just as sassy as my ex. I had to be drunk! I locked the bedroom door, hopped in the bed, and passed out until morning.

Chapter 18
The Reception

I walked into the hotel lobby. A massive revolving door spun round and let in bursts of cool air from the outside world. I stood contra post and dodged the wind's tickle. My weekend was remarkable, but it was approaching its close. I had fourteen hours to get all of my nostalgia out.

The bachelor party was bananas. I woke up with the mother of hangovers. I spent the better part of the morning fast asleep in Josh's hotel room, trying not to puke. I lost hours trying to recover, but it was all worth it!

As I walked through the lobby of the hotel, I looked for signage that would instruct me where to go. The reunion committee said that red and blue signs would be posted everywhere. It was our farewell reception. It was the final event on the itinerary, out last chance to see one another before we all tackled the next ten years of our lives. I wanted to go out with a bang.

"Hey, Sean!"

I turned around.

"Jeannette! We sure picked a great committee president."

I tried to flatter her with kudos. She really came through for the alumni. She stayed busy the entire weekend. I never saw her frazzled. As guests came into the hotel, she directed them to the correct banquet hall.

"This place is remarkable, Jeannette. You did the damn thang! Where have you been hiding? I haven't seen you all weekend."

"Well I've seen you, Mr. Life of the Party."

"Uh oh! What's that supposed to mean?"

"I heard about Josh's bachelor party, Sean?"

"Oh my God, it was legendary! Half the men from our graduating class came! I didn't wake up until eleven thirty this morning!"

"It sounds like you guys had fun."

"We did. Where am I supposed to go?"

" You are going to walk down the hallway and look for the large banquet room on the left. You will see a bunch of poster boards and signs."

"Okay then. Well, you take care!"

"You too, Sean. By the way, Jade was looking for you."

"She was? She's here?"

"Yeah, she looks beautiful too. She should be inside."

"I will take a look."

"I almost forgot, Sean, you better make sure I get some tickets to your play when it comes to Chicago."

"I'll take care of you."

I walked down the hallway to the side entrance of the hotel. The rich furnishings, bright whites, and warm lavenders caressed the cold chrome accents on the modern décor. The hotel really took its time with the design. On the walls hung artwork from all over the world, they were all so captivating and beautiful. On the inside of the ballroom, contemporary sculptures commanded my attention with their edgy themes and impetuous mediums. One could argue that the hotel was more of a museum than a banquet hall. Every piece was placed in the perfect spot. The hotel was phenomenal. Everything was.

There were nice hotels back in Dallas, but nothing like the one we hosted our reception. Its ambiance was consummate.

I was nervous. Jade and I took it a little too far at the bar after the softball game. I didn't know how she would respond to me. We took things way too far for two people that were supposed to just be friends. We could not control ourselves. We were one another's air last night. We could breathe again. We kissed for what seemed like eternity. Our bodies craved one another.

Nothing was supposed to happen. Jade and I were only supposed to have a few drinks, chat over old times, and then call it a night. Things didn't happen that way. We both went to empty trash bags in the alley behind the sports bar and one thing led to another. We were supposed to go our separate ways, but we could not resist one another. The two tequila shots didn't help either. That liquor slapped our asses!

I barely remember the events that lead up to our very special, yet awkward, moment. Jade tried to pretend that the kiss was no big deal, but I knew better. Hugging her close and having the chance to kiss her lips once more was a dream come true. I held her hands, pulled her close, and just like that, one thing lead to another. We groped each other as if we were back in high school in my mother's car parked at the lakefront. She smelled just as sweet as she did that night.

I was a nervous wreck! I adjusted my necktie and repositioned my cufflinks to ensure that they shined whenever the light bounced off them. I went into the bathroom, looked at myself in the mirror, and made sure everything was in place. I checked my breath for freshness and spot-checked my teeth to see if I had any food stuck in between. They were pearly white. I looked down at my slacks and made sure my creases were visible. I gave my shirt a once over and made sure it was free of lint, wrinkles, or any unsightly food stains. Everything had to be perfect for Jade.

I rehearsed what I would say to her when we were face to face. I looked at my reflection in the mirror to be sure my face looked sincere. I no longer hid it from myself; I was still in love with Jade. She was the real reason I flew back home. She was the missing ingredient in my life. Not a day passed where I did not think of her. The last few days in Chicago showed me see just how discontented I was with Eva. Leaving her was the best move I could have made. Jade made me happy. She made me smile. She made me believe in myself. I wasn't ready to be with her before, but I had become a different man. I was ready, but was it too late? Although I had one last evening in town, my flight was scheduled to leave Chicago first thing in the morning. I refused to embrace time. I could not chance never seeing her again. I had to risk it all. Even though ten years had passed, my feelings were still in tact.

I had to stop worrying. The better part of my judgment told me to let things flow. I had excellent champagne and a fine meal waiting for me at my table. Worrying could wait; I'd deal with complex emotions later. The mirror returned a reflection I was pleased with, I wondered if life would ever be as sweet. Would I ever feel as carefree and as optimistic about life and love?

I popped my collar and put on my nametag then found the table I was assigned to. Each table had special seating arrangements. Alum's and their respective companions were given place settings. There was plenty of room.

I looked down at the table list to see if I remembered any of the names, but I didn't. There was one name on the list that made me smile, Jade Brown. I looked at the list to see if the box that read *guest* was checked, and it was not. She was alone. I sat down at the table. Most of the seats were empty, but a few were filled. Kensor High's Class Clown, Perry Stenson, and his beautiful companion were seated and waiting on the first course. They looked great together. Perry and his date had on matching outfits that were tasteful and fun. The periwinkle colored material looked expensive. They coordinated the blues with off white accessories. They looked like they were in love.

I grew frustrated, it seemed like everybody, except for me, was hitched. I was mildly jealous at their happiness but not enough to be salty about it. I didn't want to turn into one of those characters you see on soap opera's complaining about how nobody loves them.

Perry and his mate were lovey-dovey. They sat there gazing into one another's eyes. Their affection looked genuine. I wondered if people saw the same thing when I stared into Jade's eyes. I announced myself.

"What's going on, Perry?"

"Hey, my brother, how have you been? It's good to see you again after all of these years."

"Same here."

"Baby, I have someone I want you to meet. Brianna, this is a good friend of mine named Sean. Sean, this is my wife Brianna."

"It is a pleasure to meet you, Brianna. You guys look great! Nice outfits."

"Baby, he wrote the book I let you borrow last week."

"This is Sean Jiles? Oh my, what a pleasure to mee you. I absolutely love that book of yours. It is a real page turner."

"Thank you. I am glad you are enjoying the book."

"I am. It has claimed a place on my personal top five list. If I would have known you were coming, I would have brought the book for you to sign."

"Hey, hey, hey now…enough already, you are making me feel like I have to throw up."

Perry couldn't resist. He joked with his wife harmlessly. He meant nothing by it. I guess the class clown in him couldn't resist.

"Perry, you are still funny. You always did have a great sense of humor."

"Always. Sometimes all you can do is smile."

We all glanced at the ceremony program and the dinner menu to see what the carte du jour was. I stared at the empty seat that had Jade's nametag on it. I remembered when Jeannette said that Jade was looking for me. We were well into the second course, but there was no sign of her.

Then I glanced over to the banquet hall entryway and saw Jade. She looked spectacular. Her dress was fire engine red with spaghetti straps. that the dress fit her extraordinarily. I watched her walk to the registration desk and then back into the room. I stared at her as she walked over to the table.

"Hello, Sean."

I was thunderstruck. I had bowled over so bad that I nearly forgot to speak back to her. Perry spoke for me.

"Hey, Jade, it's good to see you again after all of these years."

"At least somebody still has their manners. Looks like somebody is still upset about losing a softball game to a bunch of girls."

I smiled at her then spoke while getting up out of my seat to pull her chair out for her. I could not help but notice her well-defined back and lower torso. Her arms were toned, and that juicy ass of hers nearly poked out from underneath her gown. Her dress looked like it was painted on.. I joked back with her.

"I'm not upset. It's just that you look so amazing, I had to catch my breath. Give yourself more credit. From where *I'm* standing, you're aren't a girl at all. You are one hundred percent woman."

"Thank you, Sean."

Jade smiled at my charm,

"Come on you two, we are trying to eat over. I can't deal with hearing y'all flirting with one another all night. Get a room!"

"We might," Jade said under her breath. I thought the same thing in my mind. I wondered if she knew I heard what she whispered. Perry knew about my past with Jade. He knew that we were still hot for one another. Yesterday proved it. I retorted.

"You're right, Perry. I will try to go easy on the cheesy compliments."

"I didn't think it was cheesy," said Jade in a seductive tone.

"Neither did I!"

Perry's wife popped him upside his head and told him that he needed to quit hating and leave well enough alone.

"I think it's cute. Don't worry about Perry, I know how to shut him up. I have that all taken care of."

"Thank you very much!" Perry said while blushing.

He knew that if he kept his mouth quiet, he could possibly get lucky later on that night. He shut his mouth.

For the next hour, we enjoyed the five-course dinner. We watched a slide show with old photos from back in the day. They had everything from homecoming day to prom night. The graduating class sipped their favorite drinks and took in the moment. We knew that the reception was coming to a close.

Perry spoke again.

"So are you guys going to Dre's afterparty?"

"Dre is having an after party?" I responded.

"Hell yeah. He put it together yesterday. It should be nice. You two should go.

Perry was trying to hint at me.

"Do you want to go to the party with me Jade?"

"I would love to."

Real partygoers know that real partying happens at the after party. Champagne and filet mignon was nice, but some Hennessy and Reggae music always hit the spot.

Dre Calhoun was a master club promoter. Everyone in Chicago knew Dre. He was the best at getting people together for a good time. He had a handful of ritzy clubs in his back pocket, and as a gift to our class, he secured the hottest club in the city, *Circus Rush*, for the official after party.

The club had a carnival theme complete with ringmaster, wild animals, and sexy clowns.. Each guest also received the

VIP treatment. I had to know if Perry planned on going so I asked him.

"Are you going to be at the party, Perry?"

"Maybe, maybe not."

"See, now why are you going to be like that?'

"You don't need me there to have a good time, Sean."

"Aiight then, Perry, you take care, brother. Don't hurt yourself.

The banquet hall closed, and I raced to my car. I undocked the convertible top and sped out of my parking spot. Since Jade drove, we took separate cars. Jade and I talked to each other on our cell phones the entire time. We flirted with each other even more. By the end of my ride, I had a boner. I made it to the club safely and used valet to park my car. I gave the attendant a twenty-dollar bill and asked him to take care of the car. I

I felt like Jade and I were at Winter Ball again.

Chapter 19
The Afterparty

I walked through the VIP entrance. A velvet rope separated the Kensor party from the general one. I saw a large poster with the Kensor High logo on it. We were running shit that night!

"What's crackin', Sean?"

I turned around and it was Dre. He had on a purple crushed velvet blazer with cursive monogrammed stitching on the back that read *The Chancellor*.

"What's up, Dre? You definitely put it down tonight. The party is jumpin'. You get all the cool points for putting this together. I have never seen anything like this before in my life. Was that a white tiger I saw caged by the front door?"

"Oh yeah, that's Lucky; he's from Africa"

"I know you had pull in Chicago, but now you have connections in Africa?

"I am just doing my thang, homie!"

"I see, I'll see you out there, family! You are the man tonight."

"What are you drinkin' on tonight? I will have one of the waitresses bring it over to your table."

"Hmm, let me think. I'll have a bottle of that Brown."

"Henno?"

"Nah, I am going to keep it simple tonight. I'll take Jack Daniels."

"Coming right up. And oh yeah, Sean..."

"Yeah?"

"When you have that production party for the stage play, remember to holla at cha boy. You know I'll keep it one hundred for you."

"You got yourself a deal, Dre."

Dre took me to the far back corner of the club near the flashing lights that lit up the dance floor. I almost had a seizure from the flickering strobes. Waiting there at the table was Jade. She must have driven like a speed racer to make it to the club before me.

"Wow...what a surprise. To what do I owe this honor, Ms. Jade?" I joked.

"Are you really surprised, Mr. Jiles?"

"A little bit. I know I left the reception before you."

"Maybe I took a shortcut."

"Jade, you still look amazing. I am so happy that you decided to come."

"Same here. Even though it's been ten years, it all seems so familiar to me."

"Are you comfortable?"

"Yes. I feel wonderful, Sean."

I sat down and contemplated my next set of statements. I built my nerve up and started asking the real questions. I put it all on the line.

"Jade, we need to talk."

I poured us both double shots, added a little bit of cola and a twist of lime to the concoction, then handed one of the drinks to Jade.

"Before I say what I have to say, I want to toast."

"What are we toasting to?"

"Let's toast to possibility."

"What possibility, Sean?"

"Jade, I am so happy that you are here with me. I have missed you so much. Truth be told, *you* are the main reason I decided to come to the reunion."

"Really, well I--"

"Baby, wait, I have to get this out while I have the nerve."

"Okay."

"Jade, I have waited ten years to tell you what I am about to tell you, and I need to make sure that you hear me. Don't just listen; I want you to truly hear."

"Okay, baby, let it out."

Jade sat there at full attention. Even though the music was loud and the flashing lights hid our faces from one another, we sustained eye contact. I looked deep into those beautiful brown eyes and continued.

"Jade, I have thought about you at least once every day for the last ten years. I understand that's a long time, and although we may be a little different now, fundamentally we are still very much the same. I still have photos of us in my apartment. Every weekend I sat in front of my computer screen wondering how you were, and if you were happy. I'm not happy unless I'm with you. Looking at a picture was one thing, but seeing you at the picnic and even now is a completely different feeling. You still take my breath away."

I poured my heart out to her. I had nothing to lose. I wanted to rewrite my future. Eva was a non-issue. She would not dictate my moves any longer. I continued to profess my affections toward Jade.

"When I graduated college, my life got turned upside down. There were times I didn't recognize myself in the mirror. It was as if I had become a lesser version of myself. I know I've made mistakes in the past. I should have valued you more. I should have been there to support you. I wasn't ready for the type of love you offered me so long ago.

Jade began to cry. She grabbed my hand and held on to it.

"We've shared everything together and you have always supported me. You were there for my first novel and my first play. You were the first person that I ever made love to. I am not afraid anymore. I should have never let you walk out of my life. I should have never let you leave me. Letting you disappear without a fight is the only regret I have ever had in my life. I have *always* loved you, and I love you still. I know now that you are the *only* woman that I have ever truly loved."

I got up out of my chair and embraced Jade. I gave her the tightest hug that I could and told her more about how I felt.

"Jade, when things fell apart, I couldn't eat, couldn't sleep, and I lost faith. I buried myself in my work and used the images of you to get through. Do you understand that I would do anything for you? I know your face so well Jade. I remember your smell, and the way you tasted when we kissed. I am dying without you; please breathe life into my soul. I believe that you were made just for me. You are everything I have ever wanted and all that I have ever prayed for. I love you."

My words were factual; I had finally let it out. It felt like a weight was lifted off my shoulders. I could breathe again. Jade and I were trapped in embrace. I held her in my arms so tightly. The ambiance grew perfect. As soon as she opened her lips to speak, "Beautiful" by MeShell Ndegeocello played softly on the speakers. All of the couples in the building rushed to the dance floor to slow dance. The music subdued us both. Jade returned a statement.

"Sean, I love you too. I have loved you since we were kids. Even though it's been a while, I know you well enough to know when you are being serious. You wrote in your first book that a person shouldn't say the words "I love you" unless they really meant them. You are my heart too, Sean. My life has been so empty without you. If you only knew."

Jade was still crying. A single tear slid down her cheekbone and fell onto the floor. As we danced, it seemed like the earth stood still. She had accepted my love. Her eyes sparkled. She looked like she had finally crossed the finish line. We were ready. I felt like I could do anything with her. I was ready to tackle the world. Jade opened her mouth and spoke back to me.

"Sean, I love you so much. When we said goodbye to each other the first time, I thought we would never see each other again. Sean, I have loved you from the first time I laid eyes on you. You are handsome, funny, generous, down to earth, and cool. Not to mention you have a brilliant mind. I read your book cover to cover looking for clues as to whether or not we still had a chance. I thought you gave up on us. When you were featured in the newspaper, I made my assistant order two copies just for me."

"Really?"

"Yes, baby. I even sent one my mother. She has always liked you. She said that you were a good man and that you always showed her respect. She said that whenever she saw you look at me, she saw the love in your eyes. That impressed her. She put the newspaper article in her box of keepsakes."

"I sent the second copy to a memorabilia company and had it made into a plaque. I still have it packaged in the box. I was about to send it to you years ago but decided against it. I figured that you were somewhere in Hollywood making movies or in Seattle signing books. I thought you erased me out of your mind."

"Why would you think that?"

"I thought that you'd be hitched by now, and I didn't want to ruin a good thing, or be a home-wrecker and get in the way of what you had. For a long time I thought you hated me."

"Hated you? How could I hate you? Please explain."

"We are both grown now, so we can talk about this. "

"Talk about what?"

"The whole sex thing."

"Oh, that thing. Jade, I knew how you felt about sex. I was just being a horny teen. I knew that you wanted to wait. I was cool with that, truly. I'm not going to lie to you, there were many nights that I went to bed frustrated as hell. Pent-up, but I made it through. I caught blue balls once or twice, but I was good."

We both began to laugh as the DJ switched gears and played an up-tempo song.

"Sean, that's what I loved about you most. You were a man of character. I always knew what to expect, even when you did something unexpected I could count on you to do the right thing. You made me feel special as a young girl. I felt wanted and desired, but you never crossed the line."

"And I never cheated."

"I know. That's what made me give up the drawers."

"What? Jade you are so silly. Are you being serious?"

"Yup."

"Do you remember the first time we made love?"

"Oh Lord how could I forget? We snuck out of the house, went to the lakefront, and had a midnight picnic. You wrote me that beautiful piece of poetry. You even read it me. You captured my mind and body that night. No man since has ever been able to do that. You did and you were just a kid back then. What a powerful love. When I went off to college, you had me up many a night fantasizing about you. Just thinkin' about making love to you had me touching myself."

"We are just telling it all tonight. Jade you are amazing."

We went back to our table and enjoyed another drink together. I started feeling tipsy.

"Be careful, Jade. If we aren't careful, we are going to end up doing something we will regret later."

"Sean, I have no regrets with you...none."

I got more and more relaxed. Jade looked like she was in bliss. We were having the time of our lives and the night was still young. Jade whispered in my ear.

"Let's get out of here."

"Where do you want to go?"

"Take me anywhere."

"Anywhere?"

"As long as you are there, I'm fine."

"I know just the place."

My hotel was a few blocks away from where the after party was. My penthouse suite had a balcony with an amazing view of the city. It even had lounge furniture and a fire pit for windy nights. It was the perfect place for us to chill. I was ready to let go and let whatever was going to happen, happen.

We left the party hand in hand. On my way out, I saw Josh near the rear exit of the club. We caught each other's eye; he gave me a thumbs-up. I knew exactly what his look meant. It was his stamp of approval. We snuck out the back door and instead of getting back into our cars we headed down the alley. As soon as we stepped foot onto the cobblestone pavement, we saw a sedan with its bright lights on at the other end of the alley. I thought nothing of it. I was too focused on Jade to care. We hurried down the alleyway giggling like two school kids with a crush. We crossed the street. My hotel was only a block away. I spoke to Jade.

"I never want to lose you again."

"Sean, I will never leave your side."

"Do you promise?"

I promise."

"We are almost there; it's just around the corner."

"Sean?"

"Yes."

"I want to make love to you."

We stopped walking and kissed each other long and hard. I tasted her sweet juices and pulled her close. I palmed her ass and felt her body quivering. I don't know if she shook because of me or the cold night air. I pressed my pelvis against her stomach and continued to French kiss her. We explored each other's mouths for what seemed like an eternity. As we stood there on the corner, I watched the crosswalk signal change. All of a sudden, a speeding car raced towards us.

HONK! HONK! BEEP! BEEP!

I looked up and saw the car heading straight for us. Instinctively, I moved Jade out of the way. I threw her body behind mine and stood chest out in front of the approaching vehicle like I was a superhero. I could not see the driver, but they were apparently drunk. A nearby cop car must have also seen the driver's erratic maneuvering, so they immediately turned on their siren and pursued the car. They driver of the compact sedan immediately hit the gas and hung a sharp left. The police chased them down.

"Are you okay, Jade?"

"Yeah, baby, are you?"

"I am fine. We damned near got hit by a car."

"Thank God we didn't. Thank you for shielding me away from danger. That was sweet of you. ."

"I just didn't want you getting hurt. Anyway, come on; follow me."

I took Jade's hand and led her down the dimly lit city block. We entered the hotel building and took the express elevator up to the penthouse level.

"Are you ready?"

"I am so ready."

Chapter 20
The Best Spy

Although I eluded the police, I should have hit Sean's ass when I had the chance. Sean and that dark-skinned bitch should be in the emergency room! I knew it! Sean had it planned since day one. If the other woman were a bust down, it wouldn't have hurt as bad. Getting your freak on behind someone's back was one thing, the connection they had was another story. They held hands like they had fallen in love.

Sean told me that he was in Chicago for the class reunion, not to rekindle an old flame. What made matters worse was that the woman he chose was the same tired ass bitch from the airport. I wondered if that bitch knew about me. Was she the reason Sean broke it off with me? Surely Sean had to make mention of me at least once at the reception. Everyone there had a date except for him and that skank!

"I'm just gonna to catch up with a few friends," he had said.

"Don't worry, I'm just gonna be in Chicago for one weekend," he had promised.

From what I saw, he did a hell of a lot more than *catching up* at the reunion. He was courting that bitch. What kind of name was Jade anyway? She didn't look oriental. She was a sister-girl.

How could he choose her? She is not as hot as I am! I was shocked that Sean was willing to sacrifice everything over her. She had no manners. I confirmed this from afar. No lawyer could dispute the visual evidence I saw from across the room. Her dress was completely wrong for her body shape. It was a Mikira Designs original, but she didn't wear it right. She looked like a stripper. In addition, the dress was fire engine red. Her dark skin looked ashy as fuck set against that color. My creamy skin would have looked much better in the dress. Sean was insane. I was definitely the better woman.

I should have known something when he turned sex down the day before he left. He *never* turned down my goodies. Sean loved getting head, but all of a sudden, he didn't me. Who cared if I was drunk? Some of the best sex happens when muthafuckas are bubbled out of their minds. To think, I was considering getting pregnant and surprising him with a baby! I must have been out of my mind. How dare he disrespect me?

Then he had the nerve to shield that bitch from my car like he was her knight in shining armor. What kind of a hold did she have on him? He never mentioned her to me, not once. He didn't have any pictures of her lying around. He didn't have old love letters, emails, or even text messages. Trust me, I looked. Sean picked the wrong bitch to play games with. I was not the one. My friends used to say that the real players were the men who could lie so good that they even convinced themselves it was true. The real heartbreakers were the men with dazzling smiles, good dick, and sneaky eyes. Those are the real threats! The men that hurt you the worst are the ones you care for.

The look on his face said it all; he was in love. His best friend Josh, with his goofy looking ass, couldn't hide his smirk well enough. I saw the satisfaction in his eyes every time he looked at the two of them kissing each other.

It's cool, because I have something in store for him that he'll never forget! Sean had no idea what I was capable of! I refuse to become some footnote in his memoirs. No way, I am not the one. I have too much pride to let Sean fuck me over.

I have bank account numbers, access codes, spare keys, passwords, copies of his hard drive, and even hidden webcams in his apartments. If he is not careful, I will sick one of my police friends on his ass. He picked the wrong bitch to play games with! Sean should have asked God about me. I was going to make him regret ever meeting me.

I had my doubts, after all Sean was still a man. Men lie, they cheat, and lead double lives. I was fed up with Sean not following my lead. All I wanted was the best for him. I told him to stay in Dallas, but he left! I knew that those vultures would be all over him. He was too stupid to see the signs like I saw them. Damn him!

I pulled over to a side street and parked. I whipped out my cell phone and called one of the tricks I used to service back at in Dallas. He was a doctor, and he gave me the hookup on any kind of prescription medication I needed. No questions asked. Whenever we fucked, the good doctor gave me pills. Sometimes I didn't even have to ask for them. The doctor was addicted to pain killers, and I loved anti-depressants. We got high together all the time. Sean didn't know about the drugs. Since I never overdid it, he never noticed. When I got high, I played it cool. I kept my pills in a tic-tac candy box. I popped pills and nobody knew. I even had a stash in Sean's place. I cut a small hole in the wall behind his refrigerator and stuffed my tablets there. Sean never suspected a thing.

My client always answered my calls, even when it was late. He never failed me. I dialed his number.

"Hello."

"Eva, hello my little sex kitten. Are you feeling freaky tonight?"

"I'm not calling about that."

"I'll pay you twice what I normally pay. Come on through. I have some pick-me-ups over here that I know you will just love."

"I said I'm not calling about that muthafucker. I want you to write me a script."

"Just come on by, I have your usual stuff here already."

"I'm not in Texas; I'm in Chicago."

"What are you doing in Chicago?"

"That's none of your damn business. Look, do I need to write a letter to the FDA telling them how you make side money. I'm sure they would love to find out which doctor is giving all of the athletes their goodies."

"Okay, I understand. What do you need?"

I texted him my request, and he faxed the prescription over to the pharmacy with light speed. All I had to do was go to the counter and pick it up. Sean was going to pay. He was mine to have. He wasn't getting rid of me!

I walked into the pharmacy, marched down the aisle, and asked for my prescription.

"Welcome to CGS Pharmacy. My name is Saamir; how can I help you?"

"A pick up for E. Sparks please."

"May I have your full name?"

"No problem. My first name is Eva."

"Thank you. So what are you picking up this evening?"

"I had my colleague from back home call in a prescription for me. It is for two medications. One is called Dilocaine and the other is Slumbearien. They should have called it in about ten minutes ago."

"Okay. Let me check my computer."

"Thanks."

I sat there waiting to see if my boy toy had come through for me yet again. I stood there trying to look professional at midnight. The pharmacy agent returned and spoke to me.

"There it is; I've found it."

"Wonderful. Can you package it up quickly and give it to me? I am parked in a loading zone, and I have about five more minutes before I get towed," I lied.

My car was at a meter and in no present sight of danger.

"Hmm, this is strange," the foreign clerk nervously uttered as he mumbled to me in a heavy accent.

"Strange? What's strange, sir?"

"Pardon me for asking, but what is this medication going to be used for?"

"Excuse me!"

The jig was about to be up. I had to flip bitch mode on and talk my meds out of his hands. I was up for the challenge. My mouthpiece was remarkable. By the looks of him, the poor man was obviously lonely. He couldn't have had a girlfriend, let alone a sex life. I used my art of seduction to demolish his uneasiness.

190

He safeguarded my meds like they were blood diamonds. I opened my blouse, let my hair down and puckered out my lips to begin my falsehood.

"Mister, I'm sorry for yelling at you. You didn't deserve that. It's just that I've had a very long day at the University. I have taught lecture after lecture and I am tired. Who knew cell research was as popular as it is? My days have been full for weeks. I really need my scripts so I can run the rest of my tests and get back home to Texas."

The clerk brightened up immediately having heard the word Texas. Before I walked up to the counter, I noticed that he had his degree proudly posted up on the wall behind him. He had received his degree from Texas Medical University in Austin. Having frequented there for sex business, I got to know the campus well. I used his alma mater in my deception.

"You teach at Texas Medical?"

"Yessir. I am doing a fellowship at TMU."

"Really! Wow! That is my alma mater."

"What a small world! When did you graduate?" I asked convincingly.

"I graduated earlier this year. This is my first job practicing."

"Well congratulations. How are those student loans coming?"

"Oh God, please don't remind me. I owe the government so much money right now."

"Well, sir, don't feel bad. I have been out of school almost five years, and I stil owe money. You'll pay it down eventually. Give it time."

"Thanks for the vote of confidence, ma'am. Now...where were we?"

"You were pulling up my information in your computer."

"Oh yeah, I'm sorry for intruding. It's just that, well, as you probably know, one of the medications is a local anesthetic. We usually sell that medication via direct shipping from the warehouse. No one ever picks it up from the store. It's a numbing agent."

I interjected to boast my limited knowledge of remedies.

"Yes, I know. Surgeons use it mostly. They take a syringe and administer it locally to help block a patient's receptors. Emergency Room doctors use it during surgery."

"Yes, ma'am, you are right. Are you a surgeon?"

"It's doctor, and no, I'm not a surgeon, not any more. Now I teach."

"That's fascinating. I show that the other medication is a sleep agent."

The clerk continued to test me. I retorted vehemently.

"Yessir, *actually* it's more of a muscle relaxer, but who's keeping score."

"Thank you, ma'am, I mean doctor."

"You're welcome."

"Let me go to the back and get your meds."

Chapter 21

Secrets of the Heart

Jade and I stood in front of my hotel door looking at one another.

"Jade, before we go inside, I need you to know something."

"You can tell me anything, Sean."

"I need you to know that I never thought I could feel like this again. I am so blessed to have you in my life again."

"I'm happy too, Sean. Even though we both have lots going on, all that matters to me right now is you. We wasted so much time."

"We've wasted too much time."

"You've got that right."

A comfortable silence filled the space. I opened the suite door and walked in with my lover. Jade moved in closer and kissed me. It felt so good. Her mouth tasted like vanilla and honey. I pulled her close and smelled the nape of her neck. Her body called out to me. I started rubbing her breasts, and she unbuttoned my shirt to expose my chest.

"Jade, wait…"

"What's wrong?"

"I need to be honest with you about something else. It may change how you feel about me. It may ruin the moment."

193

"Nothing can make me feel differently about you, Sean, nothing."

"Just let me get this out."

"Okay."

"We walked inside the room. I sat Jade on the chaise lounge and removed her heels. I massaged her feet softly and took her purse. I escorted Jade out to the terrace and wrapped her in a blanket.

"Have you ever seen anything so beautiful?"

"Never. As a little girl, I used to dream about looking at the city like this. The view is marvelous!"

"Thank you."

"For what?"

"For being here with me."

"Sean, there is no other place on earth I'd rather be right now."

"Okay, here goes."

"Spill the beans, Sean."

"I was just involved in a relationship. Up until a few days ago, I was actually seeing someone back home. I'm not married or anything like that, but we were pretty serious."

"Please explain."

"I met her in college. Her name is Eva. We dated for a year, and then one day I realized that I was unhappy with her, so I broke it off. I felt so empty with her. During our time together, we had unnecessary issues. We argued and fought all the time. I cared about her, but I didn't love her. I want to be with you."

"Sean, is that all? You had me thinking you were dying of cancer or something."

"You understand?"

"Of course I understand. I was in a relationship like that once before too. Those kinds of connections are so unhealthy. They make you question who you are as a person, and make you wonder if you actually deserve to be happy at all. I know the feeling all too well."

"I'm not worried about Eva. All I care about is you, Sean."

"I'll be right back."

I gave Jade a pillow and propped up her feet. I used the blanket to tuck her into the chair. Jade was in relax-mode. I went into the kitchen area of the room, brewed a pot of coffee, and set aside two mugs. I retrieved a manila envelope from my suitcase and took it outside with me. I handed it to Jade.

"Sean, what's this?"

"It's an envelope, silly. Open it up and see, nosey rosy."

"Boy, I am gonna bust you. I see you have developed a bit of a smart mouth being down there in Texas."

"You know I won't change, so get used to it."

Jade opened the envelope and her jaw dropped. Inside of the large envelope was the completed manuscript for my first stage play.

"Sean, is this what I think it is?"

"Yup. It's my final manuscript. I finished it early this morning. It is the complete version of the play I've been working on for the last few years. It's called *L'Amour Perdu*. I will begin casting in three weeks."

Jade was the first person I had shown the manuscript. She sat there in amazement holding my life's work. The culmination of all my pain, struggle, hopes, dreams, and all that I've wanted. It was a testament to all that I've learned, all that I have lost, and to everything I've ever loved. It sat in the palms of her hands.

"What does the title mean, Sean?"

"It's French for *Lost Love.*"

Jade stood upright, looked me in the eye, and kissed me again. The coffee machine interrupted us. The loud beeping sound signaled that the brew was ready. I left Jade on the balcony and went back inside to retrieve our dry roast. I brought the delicious cups of coffee back out to the patio and sat down on the recliner. Jade snuggled into my chest.

She tore open the envelope and read the cover page. She read the title in her best French impersonation. She began reading feverishly. The synopsis appealed to her. The storyline intrigued her. Jade smiled and looked up at me with excitement.

The play's main character was named after me. He was a successful author that received an invitation to attend his ten-year class reunion. The main character writes bestseller after bestseller but never truly finds happiness because something is missing. The main character knows what it is; he misses the woman left behind. The main character's love interest is his high school sweetheart, Ebony. Aside from being in a relationship herself, she lived across country, was a workaholic, and stayed preoccupied with a busy schedule. Sean broke her heart when they were teenagers. He chose to run the streets and focus on his work instead of cultivating their love.

Jade loved the concept. She said that everyone liked stories about people who missed love because of the demands of their career. I ran my fingers through her hair, and she read further. The synopsis went on to explain how the main character travelled back to his hometown to attend his class reunion. To his surprise, he reconnected with his sweetheart. Only falling back in love was not so easy. Both characters had baggage, but their love prevailed. All is right with the world until the twist unfurls. At the height of their elation, Ebony reveals that she is dying from cancer and only has a few months left to live.

Her only hope of survival is to receive a kidney transplant. Her chances seem bleak but at the precise moment that she is ready to relinquish hope, the love of her life bestows the ultimate gift to her. He gave her life. Sean donates one of his kidneys to her, and she survives the ordeal. However, Sean dies from the complications.

Jade took a break from reading and wiped the tears from her face.

"Are you okay, Jade?"

"I'm fine. It's just that your manuscript is so beautiful."

"Thank you."

"Please hold me again."

I walked over to her and wrapped my arms around her waist. She threw her arms around my neck and we gazed into one another's eyes yet again. I took my index finger and placed it on the undercarriage of her chin then lifted her face up to mine. Our lips were centimeters apart. I could smell her essence from within. I picked her up so that her toes no longer touched the floor. We embraced and held on to each other for what seemed like forever.

"Too bad it has to end."

"Are you talking about my play or this night?"

"Both."

"Jade, what time does your flight leave tomorrow?"
"Eight o'clock in the morning. What about yours?"
"Mine leaves at ten o'clock."
"It's already two a.m."
"I wish I knew how to stop time."
"It's cool, baby. Don't worry; let's just enjoy tonight."
"Yeah, let's make it special."

.

Chapter 22

Right Next Door

I confirmed it! Sean was cheating on me. I didn't actually see Sean walk into his room with her, but I could hear the moans and sighs of ecstasy coming from inside. I hid in the hallway and tried to pry Sean's room door open.

"Excuse me, may I help you, ma am?"

A middle-aged housekeeper came out of the suite next to Sean's and questioned me. Apparently, she was done with her shift and on her way out of the building when she saw me. She witnessed about three seconds of my snooping. I must have looked like a security risk, because she reached for her radio. I stopped her from calling it in.

"Oh, I'm so sorry. No, I'm okay. I was just checking on my Yorkie. This is her first time in the big city, and last night she wasn't feeling so well. I thought that before I went down to the bar for a nightcap, I'd check on her. How are you doing? You look like had a long day."

The woman in the uniform spoke back to me in a heavy accent that sounded Russian.

"Thank you for clarifying. Yes, yes, I am exhausted. I have been working double shifts for nearly a month. I am tired, but I must go on because I have to pay for my son's college. Do you have any children?"

I had her convinced.

"Yes, I do. A little girl; she is only eight though. College is a long way away."

"Yes, but you must prepare early. They grow up so fast."

As much as I liked shooting the breeze with the cleaning lady, I needed to get into Sean's room. Her stocky ass wouldn't shut up. We were right outside of Sean's room, and we were loud. He could have walked out at any moment or saw me through the peephole. My cover would have been blown.

"I admire all of your hard work and what you are trying to do for your son. You are a great mother. I can only hope to be like you one day."

I reached into my purse, pulled out a crisp one hundred dollar bill, and gave it to her so that the bitch would shut up.

"Thank you; thank you," the woman said at full tone.

She began to irk me with her loud ass tone of voice. I responded quickly and quietly.

"No problem. It's the least I can do, but hey, can you keep it down? I think my puppy is asleep, and we may wake her with our loud conversation."

The woman agreed. She whispered back to me graciously then walked away.

As the door was closing I wedged the tip of my heel into the closing entryway and walked inside the spotless suite. I was right next door to Sean's room. I was in a safe zone. No one would reserve a room this late. I walked around in the room and made myself at home. I put a glass against the wall and tried to listen to Sean's conversations, but I could not hear anything. I went outside on the balcony in frustration then I noticed that the balconies were constructed right alongside one another. They were literally side-by-side. Although I could not see it to confirm it, I had the nagging suspicion that Sean was next door fucking that tramp. I heard moans and hollering. My mistrust was confirmed. I had to step in.

While on the balcony, I tried my damndest to sneak a peek into the room next door, but I could not see through the drapery. All I saw were silhouettes. I could vaguely see real body parts. I knew Sean's body like the back of my hand. I could spot Sean's body in a crowd. That shiny bald-head of his and that broad chest were dead giveaways. The woman was harder to see. Was she the bitch I saw him running down the street with? I wanted her head on a plate. That bastard was up to no good. He needed to be taught a lesson. I took off my heels and went back into the hotel room. Before stepping through the sliding balcony doors, I looked over to the adjacent terrace once more and made mental measurements of the distance between my balcony and his. It looked to be about two and a half feet away. That was close enough for me to jump. I stepped back onto the luxurious cut pile carpet. I walked over to the bed and took the small paper bag filled with drugs out of my purse. I also removed the mini-syringe that came with the medication. I tore open the packaging, threw the loose casings on the floor, and filled the needle with the liquid from the small bottle. I took the sleep agent pills to the bar counter and poured them all out into a small crystal glass. I used a nearby stirring spoon to grind down each pill to a soft powder. Once finished, I poured the powder into a coffee filter and twisted it tight. It looked like I made my own bullets, except they were white. I stuffed the powder inside my bra. It was safe and secure in between my bosom. I put the cap back on the needle and secured it snuggly with my fist.

I gathered all of my things and stuffed them into a small plastic bag that should have been used to hold ice. Once all of my belongings were in place, I took one final look at the room to make sure it was still in order. I made sure that the changes I made to the room were not infinitesimal to a common eye. Only a complete neat freak could have noticed the things that were out of place.

I walked back out onto the balcony with all of my belongings. The terrace had to be at least two hundred feet in the air. We were more than twenty stories up. The patio sliding door closed, and I heard a clicking sound. There was an electronic keypad that lit up. It had a keypad on the dial and required either a code or the rood keycard to enter and exit. The door was locked and I didn't know the code. Damn! I was stuck out there. Even if I wanted to change my mind, there was no turning back. I was pissed.

Sean was the one that needed to be afraid. He and his new fuck-buddy were in store for a night they would never forget. I built up my nerve then walked over to the edge of the terrace. I quietly tossed my bag of effects to the other balcony. It landed on the base of the terrace floor with no sound. I pulled my skirt up, counted to three, then climbed onto the terrace railing. I was on a mission of hate. My eyes were pierced with revenge. I secured my footing and made my leap. My heart was cold.

I landed on my feet like a black cat. I lost my left hoop earring, but I was safe. The nighttime air whistled. I stood upright, hid behind the blind spot on the balcony, and waited patiently. I readied myself for sabotage and saw that the balcony door was not only unlocked, the patio door was half opened. I took the cap off my syringe and took the coffee filter filled with powder out of my brassier. I was ready. I walked over to the door, took a deep breath, and placed my hand on the door handle.

Chapter 23

The Confrontation

"Surprise! Where did you hide that ditsy ass broad?"

"What the hell!"

My eyeballs nearly popped out of their sockets. Eva was standing near the sliding doors of my room. I was shocked, frightened, distressed, and stunned all at the same time. How did she get in? Eva must have been related to Houdini.

"What the hell is going on? Why are you here, in Chicago? Better yet, answer this, *how* are you here?"

"See, Sean, you never know where I'm going to be."

"What is going on?"

"Do you think you can have your fun with me then just brush me off to the side like dirt? No way, Jose! You have picked the wrong bitch to play games with!"

Eva reached inside her brassiere and pulled out a needle. I really began to grow concerned, because I knew how crazy Eva was. She was unpredictable. Eva was the one woman on the planet that was capable of anything. I had to try to talk some sense into her crazy ass.

"Eva, hold on, wait a second. I can explain."

"Do you think I am a fucking fool?"

Eva lifted up her closed fist and showed me the needle. As I looked closer, I saw that it was a surgical syringe, and its basin was filled to capacity with liquid. She also pulled out a small bright pouch that looked like a stiff paper towel. It contained a powdery substance inside that seeped out onto the floor. Was she on drugs? At least that would explain her erratic behavior. She looked certifiably crazy standing there with half a dress on, smeared makeup, and a syringe cap in between her teeth.

"Eva, what are you doing?"

"Something I should have done a long time ago. You aren't gonna fuck around on me ever again! How many *other* women have there been?"

"Other women? Eva, wait…"

"Sean, don't talk to me like I am a fucking idiot. I saw her. With my own two eyes."

"You saw who?"

Eva pointed the needle at me and motioned towards me.

"I saw you cuddled up in here with that bitch. How long have you been fucking here?

"Eva, you've got the wrong idea. I know how this must look, but nothing happened. Please just give me a minute to explain."

"I saw you, Sean! I saw you at the airport, at the picnic, and at the reception. I saw the way you looked at her. I saw the way you looked into her eyes. You are in love with that bitch. You chose *her* over me! Where is she?"

"You mean to tell me that you have been in Chicago following me around like a stalker all weekend?"

Eva thought she could read me like a book. She was correct about one thing though. I was in love with another woman.

"That skeezer must have left after you ate her pussy. Did you let her suck your dick? Did she swallow your cum like I did? Did you fuck her?

"Eva, you are a maniac, a psychopath! Who in the hell are you to be accusing me of anything. I still can't believe you are in Chicago. You weren't calling me from Dallas at all! You were right here in the Chi."

"Damn skippy!"

"I don't have to explain myself to you and deal with this shit. Get the hell out of my room."

"I'm not goin' nowhere, Sean. I am gonna show you just how crazy I am!"

Eva stepped closer and looked down to the small pasty colored sack in her hands. She flung it towards my face. The white powder filled the air and all immediate space around me was painted a pallid ivory. The powder covered my face and crept into my nostrils. The floor was covered with residue. I tried to regain my composure, but uneasiness began to overcome me. I wiped the concentrate off my face and reached for my phone. Eva began to laugh.

"There is no running from me."

"Eva, wait a second. Let's just have a drink and chill for a second. We don't want to do anything that we'll regret later. Let's just relax, have us a few shots, and talk about this. Please calm the down."

Eva, a true lush, looked over to the bar area and smirked.

"Are you trying to get me drunk and take advantage of me?"

Eva sounded like a psychopath.

"I see you went out and bought some good liquor for that bitch. She ain't drinking any of this tonight. Neither are you, wit' your cheatin' ass. That liquor belongs to me; I'm gonna drink it!"

Eva put the small white bag on the bar counter and grabbed the bottle of Gin. She took the bottle straight to the head and guzzled down the remaining liquor that was left in the bottle. The bottle was only half full but she still looked like a pirate guzzling down the fluids. Eva threw the empty glass bottle against the wall and lunged at me from across the room. Her body connected with mine. We fell onto the bed and rolled around on top of the covers. She threatened to stab me with the needle. She rubbed her body against me as if we were dry fucking. With her right fist, Eva tried to bury the syringe she was holding onto into my body, but I grabbed her arm and wrestled her to the ground. We fell to the floor. Eva's eyes looked devilish. She really wanted to do my body harm. She could not control herself. I tried to reason with her nutty ass, but it a big waste of time.

"Eva! I am warning you. Put down the needle. I don't know what the fuck this is, but if you don't back off, I have no choice but to defend myself. I don't want to put my hands on you, so please stop. Right now!"

"I'm not stopping shit!"

"Eva, what do you have in that needle? What's this powder?"

"You were supposed to me mine, Sean, mine! We were supposed to be together forever. Your dick belongs to me."

"I understand."

"If I can't have you, then no one else can."

I knew Eva was hurt, but I was starting to believe that she really you wanted to see me dead than to see me with anyone else. She would never let me live in peace. Even if I did escape the predicament, could I really live the rest of my life wondering if Eva was behind every dark corner? All the signs were there and I ignored them.

Eva sank her teeth into my chest and bit me. She grabbed a huge chunk of my flesh with her teeth and chewed. She jolted her teeth from side to side. I hollered out in pain and then grabbed her neck with both of my hands. I did not want to hurt her, but she gave me no choice. Sensing a sleeper hold coming, Eva used her free hand to unbuckle my pants. She aimed the syringe at my penis and threatened to make me a girl if I did not let her go.

"Get your fucking hands off me, Sean!'

I obliged. Eva had somehow grabbed hold of my dick during the scuffle. She threatened to inject the liquid into my balls if I did not do exactly as she instructed. Eva began to command me.

"So you're giving my dick away, huh? Take off that shirt. Let me see that pretty chest."

"What!"

"Say yes, ma'am to me, you piece of shit, or you'll be pissing blood for a month.

"Yes, ma'am."

I did as I was instructed. I looked over to the clock and wondered if time could move any slower. I only needed another two minutes.

"Take my bra off and rub my titties against that dick!"

"Eva, look..."

"Do it!"

Eva applied pressure to my penis. She clinched so hard that from a distance it almost looked erect. She made me pull down my pants and strip naked. She was serious. I followed her instructions.

Eva maneuvered her body so that her pelvis was positioned directly on top of mine. I could see her bush. Her wet vagina lubricated my thighs. I began to get nervous. What was Eva's plan? Was she horny? Was she trying to scar me for life? Would she cry rape? Was she trying to rape me? Eva began grinding her bare ass onto my legs. She moaned and shook uncontrollably from orgasms.

"Do you feel that pussy shaking? Do you feel my pussy cumming for you, Sean. Eva was insane. My penis was as soft as kiwi fruit skin. I was not attracted her any longer. To top things off, I had a crazy bitch damn near raping me and cumming on my leg. I looked up at the clock. I only had another thirty seconds. Eva spoke again.

"I want to taste that dick now. I am going to swallow you down, Sean. Get that dick hard for me and shove that black pole down my throat."

Eva aimed the needle at my scrotum and used her free hand to clutch my scrotum. She grabbed my testicles, opened her mouth, and started towards me. I looked up at the clock's second hand and began counting down in my head... ten, nine, eight, seven, six, five, four, three, two, one.

Eva began losing consciousness. Her grip grew weaker by the second. The needle fell out of her hand and onto the floor. Eva's eyes rolled into the back of her head, and she could no longer piece sentences together. She fell out and flopped onto the unoccupied side of my king size bed. I caught my breath, got up off the bed, and ran into the bathroom to throw some cold water onto my face. I hobbled over to the wooden desk and powered on my cell phone. I scrolled through my contact list and found the name I searched for. I depressed the TALK button and listened to the phone ring. My party answered.

"Hey, it's me."

"Yeah."

"It worked."

"Okay, Sean, I'll make the call. Just hang tight."

"Okay, hurry. I only have four hours to do what I need to do."

"I got it."

CLICK

Chapter 24

Headed Back to Dallas

I sat in my seat motionless and waited for my waitress to bring back my order. I chose the budget breakfast that included pancakes, bacon, and a side of corned beef hash. Airport food wasn't so bad. It came with a free beverage, so I chose a sweet tea. As I sat there patiently waiting for my sustenance, I reflected on my weekend. It truly was filled with good, the bad, and ugly part. All things considered, I wouldn't have changed it one bit.

Life is all about experiences. The more you comprise, the better it is. I sunk into my seat further and let the cushion support my lumbar. My lower back and ribs appreciated it. My flight was delayed. I was supposed to be in flight, but due to setbacks, the plane wouldn't take off for forty-five minutes. I figured I'd use the time to grab a bite to eat. The restaurant was near my gate. I thought about Jade. She was probably on a flight headed back to New Orleans.

Last night with Jade was a blessing from God. I wish I hadn't had to ask her to leave so abruptly, but if she would have stayed, she would have witnessed Eva's wrath. I could let Eva ruin my future with Jade.

I should have asked Jade what airline she flew on and whether or not she was headed back home to New Orleans. I was so wrapped up in the moment that I forgot. Jade said that she. she was done with Creole living and that the jambalaya no longer tasted the same. The rainy evenings made her depressed and it was time to find a new city to call home.

Jade was always ready to pick up and go. She packed light. She had no problem bouncing around from city to city. Jade said that moving around kept things fresh and helped her keep a clear perspective. Atlanta was her top choice; she told me that Atlanta seemed like a perfect for her.

Jade's priorities were in line. Even with her recent success, she remained humble. She was *exactly* the kind of woman that I wanted by my side. With her, I could accomplish anything.

My situation was heartbreaking. The love of my life was on a plane headed to a place nine hours away from where I lived. With all the post flood work and Katrina damage, New Orleans became a turn off for Jade. Even if I flew down to see her every weekend, our conflicting schedules wouldn't give us a chance to see much of one other. How sad. My waitress brought my food and drink to me.

"Here's your breakfast and the iced tea you ordered. Do you need anything else?"

"Thank you for bringing this over so quickly. Everything looks great. I do want to make one change though."

"Sure, anything you need."

"I am having such a rough morning. The love of my life is on a plane headed to New Orleans. She was my high school sweetheart. I probably won't get a chance to see her for a while. Can you take the sweet tea back and bring me an Irish coffee with two shots of whiskey and heavy cream?"

The Reunion

"Absolutely. Coming right up."

I thought about Eva's dumb ass. She really showed her ass last night. I had never seen n explosion like hers in my life. Her performance was one for the ages. She had to be obsessed to do what she did. She was possessed.

Thank God for friends. If it had not been for the friendships I had made back in high school and a little intervention, who knows where I would have ended up. They really came through for me, on all counts. Let me explain.

It all started with my travel agent. She was a friend I knew in high school. Because we were still cool with one another, I decided to use her travel agency for all of my travel. I told her that I suspected Eva of foul play. When she booked my arrangements, she created put a special site key ID on my account that tracked all log-ins. When Eva hacked into my file, I knew about it. I was privy to Eva's deception from day one.

I saw her at the departure gate in Dallas. Who could miss her drunken ass at the bar? When she came out of that bathroom with her cleavage out, looking desperate, I saw her. When I made it to Chicago and rented my car, Charlene saved me too. She not only reactivated my reservation, she was able to get me a nicer car. Charlene tipped me off to Eva's plan by passing me a printout that contained all of my reservation's account notes. I read the section that stated the reason for cancellation. I knew that Eva planned to sabotage my reunion.

I even knew about how she tripped the emergency switch in the parking lot elevator at the hotel. What Eva didn't know was that the janitor I called to help get me out of the elevator was Josh's uncle. When I heard his name and saw his face, I told him

213

about Eva's scheme. I made a call to him, and he worked with hotel management to comp my room. Because of Eva, I was able to get a Penthouse suite.

Eva's attempts were futile. I damned near knew everyone in Chicago. I knew about Eva showing up at the picnic. I saw her stalking me from a block away in that little shit box of a car. I knew that she would never find a parking spot close enough to the park to see me in plain view. She ended up having to park near the housing projects. Eva was too stuck up to step one high and mighty foot out of her car and walk the half mile she needed to walk to get to the picnic. She must have feared for her life. Uppity people never went into the projects, but not me. I was raised in them.

I knew that Eva crashed Josh's bachelor party. She stuck out like a sore thumb. She was the only female in a room full of men with no costume on. She stooped to a new low when she went into the bedroom with Tommy and sucked him dry. Tommy couldn't keep secrets, had a bug mouth and told me everything. Back when he was a petty thief, I took the rap for him for stealing, and he owed me a favor. Back in the day, when we were both seniors in high school, he went downtown and stole a diamond watch from a high-end department store.

The cops took me in for questioning and tried to get me to rat out Tommy for stealing. The store's security said that if I led them to Tommy, they would let me off the hook, but I never ratted out my friend. I took the rap for *his* stealing while he got away scot-free. I spent four hours in a holding cell until one of my uncles came and bailed me out. Because we were both eighteen it went against our records and it cost me three hundred dollars to get it expunged.

The next day I saw Tommy at school, and he apologized. He repaid me the money I lost, went back to the store to pay for the watch and let me keep the timepiece for being a good friend. He was so grateful. He said that if he had been caught, he would have been sent upstate since he had already had two strikes for stealing. He made a promise never to steal again. He also said that he owed me a favor, and that whenever I needed to cash it in, I could call him. I still have the watch he gave me. When I saw Eva, I pointed her out to him. I told him that I needed him to push up on her to see if she was as fickle as I thought. I wanted him to test the waters and see if she would bite at his advances. Eva was no good.

Tommy left the main area of the bachelor party, got with Eva, and came back looking exhausted. He said Eva had given him a blowjob and fucked him in less than ten minutes after meeting him. He told me that although she had some bomb ass head, she was not good enough to be with a guy like me. He said that one day I would regret being with her, if I didn't cut her loose. I gave him a pound, thanked him for the dirty deed, and went to my room to catch some Z's. Security kicked the bitch out when the last guest left. I told Josh about what had happened, and he shook his head. He was glad his reservations were satisfied with Eva's whorish actions.

Eva never had the upper hand on me. I saw her at the formal reception, snooping around. She sat in the shadows and watched me interact with Jade. She tried her best to hide her humiliation, but I could see her jealousy and discontent written all over her face. I alerted Jeannette and the hotel staff that we had a party crasher. I wrote a note on a piece of paper, and they removed her

215

trifling ass right away. She never knew it I was responsible for that.

When we went to the after party, I could smell Eva's hideous perfume from the VIP section. She reached a low point when she tried to run into Jade and me with her car. I knew she was on the balcony waiting to storm into my room. The cleaning lady was actually working for me that night. She was not even on the clock. I saw her in tears in the hallway, so I talked with her. She told me about her child in college and that she could barely afford tuition costs.

I told her my name and to my surprise, she knew all about my work. I told her about Eva and that she was hell-bent on ruining my special time. I reached into my wallet and gave her a thousand dollars right then. I told her that I didn't know why, but I wanted to help her. She asked me if there was anything she could do for me to return the favor, and I asked her to be on the lookout for Eva. I told her that when she saw her to call me so I could prepare for war.

That's why I made Jade leave. I did not want Eva to harm her. Jade didn't need to be subjected to Eva's foolishness and imprudence. Jade crept out before Eva even knew she was there. Jade was better than that. She only deserved the best parts of me. When Jade left, I prepared my defense. Another Kensor alum, Saamir Burundi, helped me out the most. He was a pharmacist for CGS. If it wasn't for his presence of mind, I could have been killed. He spotted my photo inside of Jade's purse when she reached inside it to retrieve the phony prescription.

Saamir spent more than eight years in medical school learning pharmaceuticals. When Eva presented the lethal mix of drugs, he knew she was bullshitting from the jump. She asked for extra high dosages of remedies that were reserved for hospitals. He knew right away that she was up to no good. What made things worse was that the prescriptions she had in her possession were actually real. He told me that if she had strolled into *any* other pharmacy she would have been given the scripts.

Saamir and I had two classes together senior year at Kensor-- chemistry and literature. We both needed to pass those courses in order to graduate. I hated chemistry, a subject that Saamir loved. He absolutely hated literature, a subject I adored. After getting poor grades on the mid-terms, I approached Saamir and suggested that we tutor one another in our perspective weaknesses. We met at his parents' house every week and studiee hard.

At the end of the semester, we both finished with passing grades and we graduated with no problem. When Eva walked into the pharmacy and Saamir saw my photo, he called me right away. We had kept in touch over the years. He knew about Eva from our discussions.

Saamir wasn't much for fanfare, so he did not attend any of the ceremonies, but he knew about the reunion celebration. He could not attend, he had inventory to sort so he decided to work late that evening instead. Although he was a pharmacist, he worked long hours like that of a diner waitress. Saamir really made use of the degree he worked so hard to get. It pissed Saamir off knowing that there were people in the world who didn't value ethics and live with principle as he did.

Samir did not fill the prescription, he instead gave her a set of sugar pills and a bottle of purified saline solution. Eva left the pharmacy with nothing more than salt water and breath mints.

The drugs she had couldn't knock out an infant. Saamir called me and told me that Eva's actions seemed suspect. I knew her personally so I was certain that she would use foul play. He said that what Eva did was a violation of the medical doctor's oath. He was furious. Saamir researched the M.D that wrote the prescription and discovered that he actually knew him. Doctor Ulysses Berkshire III. Who could forget that name? The world was so small.

Saamir said that he and Ulysses attended the same graduate school and that he was a cheat. Saamir said that the good doctor practically swinded his way through medical school. He used his father's pull and the Berkshire family name to get him appointed. Saamir hated his guts.

Saamir said that during the last year of their doctoral studies Ulysses used Saamir's answers on the final exam and scored an A-grade. The professor reviewed both papers and noticed that all of the answers, even the written ones were the identical. The professor called a meeting and instead of coming clean, Ulysses accused Saamir of cheating. The professor, a family friend of the Berkshire's and recipient of untold amounts of donation money, sided with Ulysses. Saamir was nearly expelled from school for nothing. He had to spend an entire summer making up the course. Saamir also had to retake the final exam. He had a perfect score.

Saamir vowed get his restitution, and Eva offered him his opportunity. Not only did he give Eva phony meds, he gave me a sleeping agent that was in powder form. He instructed me to find a beverage, and as soon as the chance presented itself, dissolve the powder into one of her drinks.

The Reunion

Saamir said that if Eva drank the tainted fluid, she'd enter a deep sleep in minutes. He said that the sleep would be deep enough to allow time for me to escape her wrath. I did. Once Eva fell asleep, I took her to the elevator and called the hotel security. I complained to hotel staff and said that a prostitute was inebriated in the elevator. Last I heard, the police put her in cuffs and hauled her devious ass to jail.

Saamir also said that he had enough evidence to get his arch-rival's medical license taken away. Saamir said that he would take the phony prescription that Ulysses gave Eva to the medical board. The good doctor would soon be paddling up shit's creek. I followed his plan, and from the moment she stormed into my room, I knew exactly how she would behave. The only thing that caught me off guard was her provocative seducement. She acted like she was a sex crazed nymphomaniac. Even in all her anger, she was still overtaken by lust. Her flesh took over, and she turned into a sex fiend.

It was over, but I still didn't have Jade. I devoured my breakfast and looked down at my watch. The time read 9:50 a.m. The dream was over, and it was time for me to get on my plane.

"Southern Airlines paging all passengers for Flight 777 to Dallas with a layover in Atlanta, Georgia. We are now boarding. Please proceed to gate K52 for departure."

219

Chapter 25
Layover in ATL

I landed! My layover would be brief. Atlanta's airport was big and exciting. I could use a good stretch anyhow. I needed Jade at my side. She was the woman I was supposed to marry and spend the rest of my life with. I connected with John's words and with his advice. I ignored the signs. Jade had been calling for me all along; I just never listened.

As I walked through the terminal, I pulled out my cell phone and found Jade's phone number in my directory. I called her number and listened to the phone ring. No one answered. I hung up the phone in disappointment. I put my phone back into my pocket, but as soon as I put the phone back into my pocket, I heard a series of chimes. I had a voice message. I looked at my screen and saw that I had one message in my mailbox. I called my voicemail access number and listened to the message. It was from Jade.

"Sean, I can't stop thinking about you. I have been sitting here in the airport since this morning. I missed my flight with Southern Airlines. Damn them! The ticket clerk gave me the incorrect departure gate and I missed my plane. I could strangle her. It doesn't' matter though, All I care about is you. I wish we were together right now. I love you so much. I feel like we were given a second chance. We can't let that chance slip away. I don't know how we can make things work, but I do know that I can't live without you. Please call me. I'd love to speak with you. Since I missed my flight, I had to catch a stand-by. To make matters worse, the only stand-by flights that were left all had layovers. Guess where my layover is though…Atlanta. I always said I wanted to check out ATL. Now I have my chance. Call me; my flight doesn't leave until later this evening. I would love to hear your voice."

My heart filled up with hope knowing that Jade felt the same way that I did. She loved me just as much as I loved her. I could not believe that she and I were in the same airport! What were the odds that we would end up in the same airport on layover at the same time in the same city? We were destined. I walked through the hallway and searched for the Southern Airlines gate. I looked at the plasma screem monitors for flights headed to New Orleans that had layovers in ATL. I found her flight and her gate. I looked to the waiting area and saw her. I scrolled back through my contact list and searched for Jade's name and called her. I pressed my TALK button and listed to it ring. My heart raced. The phone rang once more then Jade answered.

"Hello. Sean, is this you?"

"Yes!"

"Did you get my message?"

"Yes."

"What do you think about it?"

"Turn around."

"What?"

"Turn around, Jade."
Jade dropped the phone. Then ran over to me.
"I love you."
"I love you, too."

Chapter 26
The Reunion

"Sean, make love to me; right here and right now," she whispered to me, and then closed her eyes. I slowly undressed her, taking my time and enjoying what I felt and saw.

"Kiss me, Sean."

Obliging her request, I kissed her passionately, and her feet left the floor, her legs wrapped tightly around my waist. I carried her to the bed. Easing her legs from around my waist, my lover unbuttoned my shirt and unfastened my belt buckle, as I reached under her dress, and caressed her thighs, before removing the red thong she wore. Impatient and wanting to feel her, I gently grazed my thumb between her thick lips.

"*Oooh shit*, baby," she moaned. "That feels *so* damn good to me," my sweetheart moaned, sounding like a love angel.

I hummed in my low register and told her how much I cared about her, my fingers now gradually stroking the inside of her. With her head thrown back, and eyes closed, she slowly worked her hips on the girth of my fingers, simulating what she would do with my dick. We kissed aggressively. I felt my nature rise. I could no longer keep my beast caged. Juices moistened my member, as tiny droplets of pre-cum oozed from my erect dick. The front of my boxers absorbed every drop, but not for long. My vixen ripped off my shirt and buttons flew everywhere, exposing my chest. She rubbed her fingernails across my pectorals.

"Look at you, Sean! You look so good to me."

"Thank you, baby, but I am nothing compared to you."

We removed every article of each other's clothing until we stood naked, taking in one another's magnificence. We stood there for what seemed like hours admiring each other's intricacies. I loved her small waistline and the way her back arched when she poked her chest out and locked her knees. Her nipples were dark and full. My black skin blended perfectly against her cocoa skin. Everything about her body was placed perfectly, even the tiny dots that surrounded her areolas. She was my princess. Her strong jaw-line and full lips complemented her face. Every time she licked her lips, I grew in anticipation. She puckered them out as if she wanted to be fed. I kissed her again.

I loved the way her lips looked on her face, as if God took extra time and drew them on Himself. The cute little mole on the right side of her face made her seem even more seductive. I wanted to taste her, feel her, kiss her, hug her and please her until she could take no more. I would make love to her until night turned into day.

She looked at me like a vulture. I was her prey. She climbed off the bed and circled me as if I was her meal. I was both confident and terrified. Was I enough for her? Could I satisfy her? Would she enjoy it as much as I would?

Stopping behind me, she leaned in close and pressed her moist lips against my back, and then ran her tongue up and down my vertebrae. She was such a mosaic with her freakiness. Wrapping her hands around my penis, she stroked me down with the pre-cum. I reached for my condoms.

"You won't need those for a while, Sean. I want to taste you. Feed me."

I was so turned on; her teasing made me throb with anticipation. Like a snake, she slithered down my body, opened her mouth and accepted me. Her warm mouth was welcoming. She teased the tip of my dick with her tongue. It felt so good. I spoke to her in an intoxicated language of adoration that was only understandable to a sex-crazed lush.

"You look so beautiful to me, baby."

"Mmmmm…You *taste* so beautiful to me."

"How does it taste?"

"Your flavor is warm and smooth like hot chocolate."

I was completely smitten with her. She had me sprung. I was every bit of hers as she was mine. I gave her permission to do anything that she wanted to me. She force-fed herself.

The thousand thread count Egyptian cotton sheets felt nice. There was little friction. My dick was granite hard. She played tag with my tool and her tongue. She swallowed my magic stick with a senseless fervor that overtook her. Covering my dick with saliva, she slid my pole in and out of her mouth, as she hummed lullabies that made me so hot for her. She deep-throated me until my scrotum tapped against her chin. She was so into it.

I watched her as she pleasured me, satisfying me to the point of feverishness. She began to shiver; her body vibrated like a pager. My darling put together a half-broken sentence in the middle of servicing me.

"Ooh shit, Sean. I'm about to cum, baby. This dick tastes so good to me. I want to feel it deep inside of me now."

Her eyes closed, and she began quivering uncontrollably. She had an orgasm. Seeing her enjoy herself threw me into a fit. I wanted to pleasure her the same way she pleasured me. I concentrated hard on holding back my ejaculation, pulling my dick out of her mouth; I had to stop her. I felt all the precursors of an orgasm coming. My dick stiffened to diamond toughness, and I began to tremble inside.

I hoisted her over my shoulder and carried her over to the nearby chaise lounge. I plopped her down as if she was a bag of rice. I forced her legs open and buried my face into her delicate folds. My tongue flickered and jabbed at her clit, while her moans let me know that I had sent her into ecstasy. I licked every portion of her inside parts and sucked hard on her clit until she could no longer take it, sending her into another vicious orgasm. She was in a euphoric bliss. The look on her face said it all. She began squeezing her breasts and clinching onto the armrest. She held on for dear life as I placed both of her hands on my baldhead. I wanted her to force feed her pussy to me.

"Am I hitting your spot, baby?"

"Yes," she managed to get out through the deep pants.

"Does it feel good to you?"

"It feels like heaven, Sean."

"Feed me your pussy, baby. Make me swallow all of your juices. I want to taste your waterfalls when you cum. I want to taste every part of you."

She hollered at the top of her lungs. I watched her as her body convulsed.

"Oh God, I am cumming for you, baby. Ooh, ooh. Can you taste my love coming down for you? Can you taste my waters flowing into your mouth, Sean?"

"Yes, I can, baby."

I loved it. Her cum tasted like peaches. She had multiple orgasms from our sexy foreplay. She pushed my head from between her legs and slid her ass closer toward my pelvis. My dick was mere inches away from her opening. I grabbed a condom off the nightstand, tore open the wrapper and rolled it on with lightning speed. Lying in a submissive position, I leaned in close and whispered into her ear.

"Baby, I love you so much. I want to enjoy every moment of this."

"Me too, Sean, I want to feel you inside of my soul, baby. We owe this moment to ourselves."

I readjusted my body. She was spread-eagle, waiting for me. As I looked at her, I visualized my rod sliding in and out of her. My dick was just the right size for her juicy love spot. I knew I was thick enough to stretch her sugar walls and stroke against her G-spot.

I grabbed her plump bottom and filled her out with my dick, her breasts sitting up on her chest and swaying from side. I nibbled on her neck and kissed her gently. She spoke to me.

"I want you to make love to me first; then I want you to fuck me."

"I love you, baby."

"I love you too, Sean."

I motioned towards her. I jabbed the tip of my penis against her clit and searched for a warm, wet home. Jade begged me to insert, but I waited. I was still. I wanted her to want me as bad as I wanted her. I needed her to crave for me.

"Put it inside of me, baby; I need to feel you."

In one action and with no stillness, I fully inserted every bit of my tool inside inch by inch. She held on for dear life. I shook vehemently from her warmth. We both took deep breaths. In unison, we uttered the same soulful sounds, only they were octaves apart. Moaning in G-sharp minor and trapped in circle of fifths, our bodies were in the same key signature. It felt so good; it felt so right. For the first five minutes, we made love, then as she instructed, we spent the rest of the time fucking. She encouraged me.

"Now I want you to fuck me, Sean. Fuck this pussy! Poke me with that fat dick."

"You better fuck me back, baby."

"Sean, I'm gonna put this pussy on you like you've never felt before."

I pinned her arms down flat against the soft sheets. Her back pressed hard against the bed. I forced myself deeper and deeper inside of her. She met my every move and pulled her legs even further apart. Soon her legs were completely behind her head. I had only seen moves like that in adult films. Her ass was propped up like candy on a shelf. Her pussy was for the taking. I had penetrated her so deeply; I could feel the labia of her vagina surrounding my balls. She covered my testicles with her sticky lotions. She loved it. We fucked for nearly thirty more minutes like two dogs in heat. She screamed and so did I. We were so into it. She yelled.

"Aaaaah! I'm about to cum!"

"Yes, baby, yes! Please, hold it right there. I'm gonna come, too."

I concentrated hard and stiffened my penis veins with every pump so that I could scathe her G-spot with every siphon. All of a sudden, she stopped breathing. Her skin was completely flush.

It looked like she was suffocating, her nostrils flared as she tried to suck in air. From the way her face looked, she appeared to be having the orgasm of her life. She was in complete convulsion.

I left my rock hard penis deep inside of her folds while she quivered on my pole.

"I want you to cum for me now, Sean?"

"Yes."

My lover climbed on top of me. I placed a pillow behind my head. She bounced up and down on my magic stick. Like a jackhammer, she rose her ass up and then plopped it down repeatedly. Her titties jiggled from left to right as she rode my dick. Every time her ass plummeted down on me, I was closer and closer to climax. Her movements were sudden and forced. She had me in a daze. I took the nearby comforter and pulled it over my face to hide my screams. She had me hollering like a goblin on Halloween. I was ready to release. She must have known it too because she started talking dirty to me.

"Do I feel good to you?"

"Yes."

"Do you love this pussy, Sean?"

"I do."

I hadn't been through a sexual hurricane like that in years. I was about to explode. She hopped off me and removed my condom, then shoved my exploding dick down her throat. She tasted me and encouraged me to fill her mouth with my semen. She wanted my essence to paint her face. She assured me that no matter where I squirted, no matter where my fluids landed, she would use her tongue to catch my juices. I could no longer hold it in.

"Baby..."

"Are you cumming for me?"

I exploded! As I leaked, my lover took in my fluids. She caressed my shaft and massaging out every drop. I was in euphoria. All of my pain, frustration, anxiety, hurt, throbbing and aches were now gone. I had never felt as satisfied in all of my life. I was exhausted. The down comforter felt like a patch of clouds.

"Sean, I love you."

"I love you, too."

All of a sudden, my cell phone rang. Half-drained and lost in the moment, I ignored it. When it rang a second time, I grew concerned. I heard my voicemail chime signal to me that I had a message waiting for me.

I got up out of the bed and reached for my phone. Yawning, I looked at the phone to see the phone number that was on my missed call list. I did not recognize it; the number was from the 312 area code. It was a Chicago number.

I called my voicemail access number and entered in my access code to retrieve my message. When the message played, I could hear commotion and conversations going on in the background. There was an initial pause, and then a female voice spoke, a voice that I couldn't forget even if I tried. It was Eva. I turned the volume of my phone down low so that Jade wouldn't hear whatever foolishness Eva left on my voicemail machine. Eva spoke.

"I just made bail, mutherfucka! You think you are the only one with friends in high places? This shit between us isn't over, Sean. It's nowhere near over. In fact, it has just begun. Trust me when I tell you this; you are going to be seeing a whole lot of me. Even though we are no longer a couple, we should at least be respectful to one another. Especially since you are going to be a father. Oops, I'm sorry; did I forget to tell you? Guess what, Sean? I'm pregnant! It's yours!"

THE END

Discussion Questions

1. What did *The Reunion* teach you about the power of love and the negative strength of jealousy?

2. In the beginning of the story, Sean said, "I chose to accept what I had, accept what I saw, and accept what I received. I settled." Have you ever settled in your relationship? In what ways?

3. Did anything in the book surprise you?

4. Why do you think Eva's relationship with Sean fell apart? What could have made it work?

5. How did Eva's conceit and arrogance blind her? In what way did it affect her relationship?

6. One theme in *The Reunion* focuses on the influence that women can have over the male consciousness. This gift can be used for good or evil. How do women use their "influences" in relationships? Are there any consequences?

7. In the story, Sean says that any woman can turn a man on by putting on a skin tight dress, make up, and heels, but it takes a "different" kind of woman to turn a man on with her mind. Has there ever been a time an attractive man/woman passed you over for an average or below average woman/man and

you thought to yourself, What do they have that I don't have? What qualities do you think they possessed?

8. What was the significance of Sean's discussion with John R.Williams-THE Author?

9. How did his words affect the way he chose to deal with Jade?

10. Why do you think the author chose not explore Eva's past in great detail?

11. What role did loyalty and friendship play in the story?

12. How did Eva use a person's weakness to her advantage?

13. Were you surprised by any of the Eva's treacheries?

14. What do you think will become of Sean and Jade's relationship? What challenges do you think they will face?

15. What are your weird high school and class reunion moments?

16. Do you think that Sean went to Chicago with the intent to reconnect with Jade? Do you think it was all premeditated?

17. Why do you think that Sean and Jade's relationship didn't work the first time around?

18. In the story, Eva tried repeatedly to sabotage Sean's reunion weekend, but each time, due to outside forces, Sean escaped

her trapped and got the best of her. Discuss a time where this has happened to you. Discuss a time your ill will against another backfired.

19. Do you think Eva is pregnant with Sean's baby? Why? Why Not?

20. What point is too late to start over in a relationship? Is rediscovering love possible?

21. Do you think there should be a *Reunion* sequel? Why or why not?

About the Author

JOHN R WILLIAMS-The Author was born and raised on the Southside of Chicago, Illinois and is the eldest of three sons. A product of a single parent home, John discovered a deep appreciation for the arts at an early age through music, poetry and writing. As a child he was exposed to both the bitter and sweet parts of life growing up in the inner city.

In 2003, John began writing informally. He wrote in a journal daily trying to perfect his writing style. His goal was to master both comedic and dramatic writing. John received no formal training in literature other than reading urban classics and masses of poetry that he usually found at book fairs and in local libraries. He studied the works of urban novelists and allowed his ability to be influenced heavily by these cutting edge authors. Over time John developed his own unique style. John used his shortcomings as a child and experiences as a young adult to shape his edgy writing style.

The stimulus for his literary aggression is oftentimes revealed in his works. If asked, john would tell you that the goal of his writing is to entertain, educate and assist with the human spirit's progression.

While pursuing a writing career he also maintained a prominent position at one of the largest Telecommunications companies in the world. His hard work brought him success as a Sales Executive. His profession afforded him the means to truly make a go at professional writing.

In 2004 when given the opportunity to explore writing, John jumped at the chance. Within his first year writing professionally John self-published two titles. His first work; a children's short story and coloring book about the bond between father and son entitled Daddy and Me was a huge success! His second work, a co-authored book, entitled *C.E.L.L Cityfolk Electronically Livin Life: The Secrets We Hide in Our Cell Phones* was an engaging endeavor with a strong storyline about three best friends living, working and playing in Chicago that expose the hidden world of wireless treachery. In 2006 John released his first independent novel entitled What Could Have Been? The Saint, The Sinner and The Attempt. It was an underground success!

John participates in both charity community events on a regular basis and attributes his love for hip-hop and the entrepreneurial spirit as his main motivators. In his free time John can be seen frequenting just about any Neo-Soul Café, poetry reading or urban hotspot in any major U.S metropolis.

Xpress Yourself Publishing

A Publisher of Fine Books

and

2008 AALAS Independent Publishing House of the Year

Visit us online:
www.xpressyourselfpublishing.org